THE FLIP SIDE OF BETRAYAL

JEAN WAIRIMU KAMINA

ACKNOWLEDGEMENTS

My sincere appreciation goes to:

- God, for giving me the opportunity to share His message with the world
- My mother, Dr. Mary Wambui Kamina, who encouraged me to come out of my cocoon of procrastination and delve deep into the literary world
- My father, Mr. Floyd Kamina Mwangi who inspired the love of books in me
- My sister-in-law Valentine Achieng Kamina, my brother Quincy Kamina for their belief in me
- My friends, Villa Magati-Mwatsama and Wanja Ngunyi as well as my extended family members for their support and encouragement
- Gabriel Dinda, Patricia Mataga and the Writers' Guild team - your guidance in the process of publishing the manuscript has been consistent and valuable
- Thomas Mwiraria, my mentor, who spurred me on to my first authorship experience by constantly giving me actionable revisions that took my manuscript to the next level

The Flip Side of Betrayal

This book unravels a puzzling paradox, a love story, and will take you through experiences from exotic countries, wrapped in sudden twists of fate. Can betrayal ever have a remedy? Is there a flip side to Betrayal? A wounded soul finds recourse in the most extraordinary ways and discovers *The Flip Side of Betrayal.*

P R O L O G U E:

Jessie was livid with rage. This could not be happening to her. Fate had indeed succeeded in twisting its cruel arm around her, sending her life into spasms of her worst nightmares.

She sunk into the big leather chair, her sobs like the first drops of rain that the ground quickly drinks in. It was six o'clock in the morning.

Thick darkness enveloped her. Sombreness soaked the air. A furnace of pain burned in her gut. Her tears flowed down her face, soaking her chest and dress. She dabbed at her eyes with a grime-covered handkerchief and pulled her dress over her beautiful, slim, dark legs.

Rays of sunlight streaked in, struggling to penetrate the seemingly impenetrable darkness in the room that was cast in shadows in some areas due to the partially opened blinds. Jessie felt as if the darkness was suffocating her. A musty scent hung in the air. It had been ages since anyone had opened the large, sliding windows.

Jessie heard a faint sound in the background, like the chiming of church bells. The sound for a second startled her before she realised it was her phone. She wondered who it could be, picking it on the tenth ring.

"Jessie, I've been calling you all morning. Where on earth have you been?" It was Samantha, her best friend.

"Sorry, I was distracted." Jessie edged, pondering over an appropriate response.

"Well, then," Samantha pressed on, "How about some shopping?"

"To-Today-y-y?"

"Yes, why not?" Samantha responded impatiently.

"Okay," Jessie conceded, a sigh escaping her. She knew it was no use saying no to Samantha when she was in an impatient mood. However, she had no idea how to get off the couch, let alone leave her house where she had been holed up for a week now.

Jessie knew she could not be in this bleak abyss forever, but getting up to fully open the blinds seemed like a gigantic task for her. She distractedly watched night peel away slowly, revealing a mauve dawn. The darkness became a silhouette of vistas.

Samantha arrived at 11:00 am. She always tried to be punctual for things that interested her, like shopping.

"Hiyo nguo imetoka mdomo wa ng'ombe?" Samantha asked Jessie as she ushered her into the house.

"Not today. Not today", Jessie internally prayed.

"You look horrible! Just horrible!" Samantha added, taking Jessie by the hands and practically shoving her in front of the first mirror she came across.

Jessie dared to look at herself in the mirror for the first time in what seemed like days. Staring back at her from the mirror was a woman wearing a dress full of wrinkles, spotting haphazard grease stains and brown smudges. It was hard to believe that the dress had once been pure white. She had not showered for three days.

Samantha left an hour later.

Jessie figured it had to do with Samantha's realisation that she was depressed. Samantha knew Jessie well enough to know that she was not okay. After her outburst, Samantha had just sat with her chatting about everything and nothing, at least that is what she thought. Samantha had felt like an annoying insect buzzing in her ears. That last part, had she mentioned something about psychological help? Mercifully, she was finally alone with her thoughts again.

Jessie did not bother to shower, open the windows or the thick black out curtains the next day. She did not have the energy as she lounged in the big leather chair. Things she once found exciting, like reading and swimming, no longer interested her. Everything felt grey and meaningless. Her Westlands apartment that once felt safe was a noose, as the darkness within her consumed her.

The previous day when Samantha had called and dropped by, Jessie had been reflecting on her past, breathing through the gut-wrenching pain, confusion and despair her life had become as memories poured unrelentingly. However, one memory kept knocking her off her feet.

"Daaarling"

She heard the voice calling out repeatedly, mocking her, plunging her mind to the beginning.

C H A P T E R 1

It had been a long time coming. Jessie deserved a holiday, especially after building a successful business from scratch. Even though her parents were wealthy enough to fund her start-up idea, Jessie preferred to struggle and create her capital. The growth of the business had been slow; several customers had conned her, running away with her beautiful clothes and hard-earned money. However, what kept her going was the motivation to succeed against all odds and her motto: *"Mgaagaa na upwa hali wali mkavu."* Her efforts birthed 'Nguo Hodari', her clothing line brand that had gained so much popularity in over just five years, allowing her to travel to different parts of the world to promote her *biashara*.

However, there were other continents she had never been to, and she was dying to explore. So, her holiday getaway was a perfect time. After a few searches on the internet and conversations with travel agents, Jessie decided to try Cambodia in South East Asia.

The day Jessie arrived in Cambodia, she waited for over an hour at the Phnom Penh airport. The driver of the hotel she was supposed to stay was running late. Cursing under her breath, muttering inaudible profanities about why hotel services in some parts of the world had to be so slow, Jessie had failed to notice the man sitting on her right until he spoke.

 "Hotel problems?" He asked, smiling, revealing a set of pearly white teeth.

"Well, err, kinda," Jessie responded, feeling flustered, as she took notice of the stranger, noticing his dark thick hair that was well cut in a fade. He could not have been older than forty. "Please tell me more," he urged, leaning towards Jessie as his eyes travelled over her, taking in her mustard top and fitting black jeans that showcased a trim waist, curvy hips and snake-skin shoes to match the outfit and her taste for finer things.

"I've been waiting here for my driver to show up and he is taking forever. This is my first time in Cambodia so I thought it would make sense to be picked up from the airport," Jessie confessed to the stranger. He had such a soft-spoken demeanour that made Jessie want to momentarily throw all the care to the wind and sob all her worries away on his broad shoulders.

"I am in the same predicament as you. New city for me too," the stranger said, echoing Jessie's sentiments as a bald, fleshy, panting man lumbered into the airport and held up a placard with her name. The placard was sliding off his chubby fingers and seemed to be about to fall any minute. His shirt hung from his protruding belly, and his cherub-like face glistened with sweat. He was panting like a dog.

On reflex, she sprang to her feet and offered her hand to her newly found friend in a farewell gesture as she clutched her suitcase with the other. He held her hand gingerly in his large one, and their eyes met and locked before he released it and said goodbye.

Jessie hurried away, a flurry of emotions bombarding her, her braids flying behind her, only pausing briefly to mouth goodbye to Mr Charming. He stood rooted to the spot as though he had turned into a pillar of salt, opening and closing his mouth like a fish.

Jessie jumped into the waiting taxi. Her nerves immediately relaxed. Soon after, they were at the Crabby Beach Hotel, and she was whistling a cheery tune. "Go tell it on the mountain, over the hills and everywhere." A Christmas song in mid-June, "that Jesus Christ is born".

Jessie unpacked and changed into a t-shirt with a lion imprinted on it. It reminded her of a live one she had seen eyeball to eyeball at the Masaai Mara. She planned to go deep-sea diving the next day plus whatever else was on the hotel's itinerary. After all, she was as free as a bird, away from the stuffy office and nerve-wracking traffic jams in Nairobi. Here, everything was at one's beck and call. Jessie ordered room service, which comprised a light supper and a cup of fresh hibiscus tea. She settled in and was soon fast asleep. Not a trace of the encounter with Mr Charming crossed her mind.

C H A P T E R 2

Jessie's hotel in Cambodia was like no other she had been to before. The interior decor in the comfortable, wood-panelled rooms was a montage of beautifully contrasting shades of grey and brown; large windows overlooked both the seaside and the mountainous countryside simultaneously - a rare phenomenon back at home.

Jessie was awake by 4:00 am, much to her disdain, as this was always a struggle on working days back home. However, her face lit up when she heard the sound of birds chirping merrily outside her window and watched the mellowing of the sun into the vastness of the sky through the enormous windows, announcing a beautiful morning-a day to delve into Cambodia.

What a beautiful morning, she thought. There was no rushing to beat the traffic jam in Nairobi, no crazy clients, no lengthy meetings. Just *holidaying*. She was determined to enjoy every bit of it.

After taking a quick shower, she slipped into a pair of comfortable cotton shorts, a sleeveless pink blouse and a pair of Maasai sandals. It was time for breakfast. Jessie enjoyed an omelette, especially fried for her by a charming chef. She washed the omelette down, two sausages and some toast with a glass of fresh passion juice.

The menu had a wide variety of local food, but Jessie did not want to be adventurous on day one. She remembered what had happened the last time she had dared to be adventurous in a strange country on day one. Jessie unknowingly ate a dish called Escargot in France, which consisted of cooked land snails. Jessie had suffered an upset stomach and was embarrassed when she had unleashed the killer contents of her gas chamber amidst a large crowd. These memories heavily influenced her decision to order continental food, which she was familiar with and confident that her body would not reject. She leaned back in her chair by the breakfast table, feeling like a python that had just swallowed a whole goat. She did not budge for the next half hour as she soaked in the early morning sunshine.

 A waiter with a friendly smile jolted her out of her reverie. His eyes sparkled, and the corners of his mouth turned upwards.

"Is there anything else you'd like Ma'am?"

His politeness was not something she was used to. Waiters in some restaurants back home were usually rude and would leave you waiting as they doggedly rushed from one customer to the other.

"No, thank you," she replied and smiled back at him as she slowly rose to her feet, mulling over the day's plans in her head. The hotel had arranged for a private van to pick her and a party of other guests up and take them to the diving expedition site. Jessie felt excited like a teenager on a first date.

The van arrived after 10:00 am. Jessie entered and squeezed her way excruciatingly slowly to the back, trying not to touch anyone. Unfortunately, this proved to be impossible, especially since she had gained quite a few extra kilos these past few months. This was an unwanted addition to her curvy figure. Jessie bumped against the other guests as she passed – much to her embarrassment. Once seated, she compared the scenario to the matatus back home, recalling how the touts packed the passengers like orbit.

"Kaeni wanne wanne kama orbit" The public transport touts popularly known as *makangas* would blurt harshly for four passengers to squeeze in a three-seater.

Her mind returned to the present, where they were on their way to the beach. It was a perfect day, with a startlingly blue sky and puffy white clouds. A cool breeze gently caressed Jessie's face. Some people in the van were singing, others chatting in excited high-pitched voices. When they arrived, an instructor handed over diving kits to everyone. It comprised a scuba unit, oxygen mask, snorkel, fins, dive vest, hoses and a wetsuit that clung to one like a second skin. The scuba unit consisted of a regulator, tank and buoyancy control device with a harness and instruments. The snorkel helped one breathe from the surface in shallow water while the oxygen tank supplied oxygen while in the deep.

The instructor, Deshane, a lean man from Jamaica with long dreadlocks, welcomed them warmly and ushered them into a pleasant air-conditioned room for a briefing before taking them for a trial run in the shallow end of a swimming pool.

One of the main goals of this session was to teach the group how to inhale underwater.

Seriously? Jessie thought to herself

However, Deshane offered a tip to make things easier. He asked everyone to put on their dive masks and practice breathing through the regulator above the water until they became comfortable with mouth-only breathing. He then asked them to lower their faces into the water while exhaling fully through the regulator.

The exercise was a success. After a thorough briefing, everyone was ready to launch out into the deep.

The ocean was a flurry of activities, the fish an array of rainbow colours. One large multi-coloured one brushed against Jessie. She resisted the urge to touch it as she remembered what the instructor had told them earlier. Objects appear thirty-three per cent closer than they are due to the diffusion of light in water.

Jessie thoroughly enjoyed the feeling of weightlessness and the freedom to move in different directions in the water. Suddenly, she started to experience another phenomenon that Deshane had shared during the briefing before they started diving- cold water immersion diuresis. This is a physiological reaction that occurs when one is surrounded by water lower than body temperature. As a result, the body speeds up the synthesis of urine, leading to an immediate urge to urinate. Jessie could not believe it, she let go and went with the flow, releasing her own hot fluid into the cooler currents around her. She made an inner vow never to tell anyone this story as it was too embarrassing and disgusting!

Her counterparts seemed to be doing well. A Nigerian man named Okonkwo was so comfortable that he drifted away from the others and seemed to meld with the water, swimming as if he had been born in the water. However, everyone else forgot to use hand signals and most of the underwater skills they had learnt. So Deshane had to take turns bringing people up to the surface to explain things again, with the except for Okonkwo, who had mysteriously disappeared.

The diving activities eventually ended. Jessie's arms hang limply by her sides. She was struggling to keep her puffy eyelids open. Her red eyes stung. She felt like they were full of sand or even chilli. She had made quite a few friends by the time they were leaving and was excitedly chatting with a young American woman named Beth. By the time they got back to the hotel, everyone was hungry and made a beeline for the restaurant. As Jessie and Beth surveyed the sea of food before them, their eyes widened. There was a wide range of seafood, prawns, crabs, grilled fish, roast chicken, sautéed vegetables and stir-fried rice.

There was uninterrupted silence for the next ten minutes as the group devoured the mouth-watering delicacies before them. The dessert was exceptional, an array of chocolate cake, jelly, custard and exotic fruits. "Life can't get any better than this," Jessie remarked as she patted her belly.

A hearty nod in agreement was all her friend could manage.

"Let's go shopping tomorrow," Beth proposed.

Jessie jumped at the idea. "Sounds great!"

"It's a date then!" Beth's face lit up like a Christmas tree.

With that, Jessie headed upstairs for a much-deserved siesta. The excitement of scuba diving and meeting new people somehow drained her. She only discovered this when her head hit the pillow. She fell asleep instantly, snoring softly into the afternoon. She was awoken by soothing music that seemed to be coming from a distance, and she wondered whether she was dreaming. It was only 3:00 pm.

Jessie went out onto the corridor and looked down onto the ground floor. She saw a brightly dressed band, all male, dressed in *sampots*, the traditional clothing in Cambodia. She donned a colourful hat and hastily left the room to join the celebration without a second thought.

Other people gathered seemed to be enjoying the band as much as she did. The music worked like a charm, and even Jessie found herself in a circle, hands in the air, gyrating rhythmically to the music.

"Pardon the pun, but it looks like you're having a ball, Cinderella." The husky female voice sounded familiar. Jessie turned sharply to see who it was.

"Didn't expect to see me again so soon after the morning's adventures, did you now?" The voice said and laughed.

"Beth! What a pleasant surprise!"

"Yeah, yeah. I was asleep too but the music was irresistible," Beth said, dancing with Jessie.

Quite a few good-looking young men surrounded them, and two simultaneously held out their hands, inviting them to dance with them. They were soon twirling and whirling around the room with an occasional dip where the ladies arched their backs, hair almost touching the ground, and the men restored them with a swift sweep back to an upright position. The music ended abruptly.

"Aaaaaaah!" The hotel guests took to their seats, albeit reluctantly. Two gentlemen introduced themselves and after a lengthy, animated conversation, the ladies excused themselves, and headed for dinner.

They had a light meal, and after wishing Beth a good evening, Jessie trudged up the stairs to her room.

She fell asleep almost as soon as her head hit the pillow and hardly stirred until six the following morning. Warm sun rays through the large windowpane by her bed fell on her cheeks. Birds chirped merrily from the leafy trees outside. Jessie smiled and opened her eyes lazily. Something within her told her this would be a perfect day. She arose and padded on her bare feet softly to the window. A breath-taking view welcomed her. It seemed as though the sky had been transformed into a rainbow of sorts- streaks of red, a layer of purple, and violet, all merged with the yellow sun as it rose. She stood there for a moment, soaking in all the beauty that nature presented.

"Thank you, God," Jessie said in reverence. "Your creation is flawless."

After, Jessie headed to the bathroom for a long luxurious, scented bath. Afterwards, she reluctantly dragged her body out and wrapped it in a thick towel. Next, she flipped through the clothes hanging in her wardrobe. She frowned as she mulled over what to wear, despite carrying a suitcase full of clothes like she would never return home. Finally, she settled on a flowery, cotton bareback dress, set off by a simple silver chain with a sky-blue pendant and matching earrings. Next, she swept up her voluminous braids and slipped on some lowheeled fashionable pumps, finishing with a touch of makeup. Jessie stepped back from the full-length mirror, nodding with satisfaction at the impeccably dressed figure she saw.

Beth was already at the breakfast table when she got there.

"You look sensational!" She exclaimed as she proceeded to make a mock catcall. "You're certainly going to get us quite some attention today, honey."

Jessie blushed. "Thanks."

The two friends chatted easily and left the hotel shortly after breakfast in a taxi. The taxi pulled in front of Vattanac Capital

Tower, a towering building right in the middle of town. Vattanac Capital Tower was thirty-nine storeys high. It was the tallest building in Phnom Penh with a five-star hotel and a shopping complex. It was shaped like the back of a dragon.

As they walked in, Jessie could feel a sense of excitement creeping inside her. First, they entered a perfume shop and were astounded at the vast assortment of designer perfumes. As Jessie already had a collection at home, while Beth seemed more taken in than she was, Jessie wandered into an adjacent area, leaving a fascinated Beth '*oohing*' and '*aah-ing*'. It was a jewellery shop with quite a rare selection of stones. She walked back and forth examining each one with starryeyed interest. It was then that she saw it. It was a petite, pure black diamond in two studs with a matching bracelet. She was too absorbed to notice the hand that slid smoothly around her neck from behind. "Don't be afraid. It's me." A male husky voice whispered in Jessie's left ear.

Jess whirled to face the voice.

"Doesn't it go perfectly with the earrings?" In his hands was a silver necklace with a black diamond pendant cut out from the same stone as the earrings. He clipped the necklace shut on the nape of Jessie's neck.

"You again!" Jessie blurted out to the stranger he had met at the airport.

"You look stunning," he offered.

"*Not so bad yourself,*" she thought.

"Err – thank you," she stammered out loud instead.

"Sorry if I frightened you," said the stranger.

"No worries," Jessie responded, trying to look composed.

"So why don't I pay for the set and then we can go get something to eat as you tell me more about where you acquired such an exquisite taste in jewellery?" he said, giving that smile that had caused her emotions to flatter the last time. .

Jessie thought the stranger was outrageous but for some reason, her tongue was glued to the roof of her mouth and she only managed a nod.

"Good. It's a done deal then. And by the way, my name is John Karanja, but you can call me John". "Jessie. Jessie Wutumu," she offered.

"Nice to meet you, again."

"There you are!" Their short-lived reverie was interrupted by an indignant Beth, in a somewhat combative pose, legs akimbo and hands on hips.

"I've practically combed the entire building looking for you."

She looked fairly baffled as she sized the pair up and down, her eyes finally settling on John who she eyed him suspiciously.

Jessie let out a nervous laugh. "Sorry, I honestly thought you'd seen me enter the next shop."

She was clearly at a loss as to how to appease her friend. The handsome now-not-so –strange man quickly came to her rescue.

"I'm John." He held out his hand and offered a benign smile. It seemed to work like a charm, melting some of the tension that had begun to build around them. John invited Beth to join them to go out to eat but she tactfully declined. She bid John and Jessie goodbye as she headed back to the hotel.

C H A P T E R 3

A wave of thoughts came crashing on Jessie's mind like a hurricane as she and John strolled side by side.

"How did this man know I was here?" she wondered. *"Was it a coincidence or has he been stalking me? He knew the exact shop I was in... Yet we only had a brief encounter at the airport ... Does he know where I am staying?"* She shivered, remembering a story she had read on social media of a woman who had been followed from a local supermarket and almost killed by her stalker. John's innocent eyes did not look anything like a murderer's. Despite her misgivings, Jessie decided to entrust herself to him.

The pair left the mall at 11:00 am and got into one of the sleek taxis conveniently parked by the sidewalk. They soon arrived at a restaurant he had selected. It was an excellent choice, Jessie observed as they made their way inside an immaculate but cosy restaurant in the heart of town. The antique furniture added an aura of mystique to the ambience.

John inquired what she wanted to order for lunch and helped her choose a meal from the long list of assorted local dishes. The waiter brought two tall glasses of fresh sugarcane juice as they settled comfortably into the plush seats of the diner. Jessie avoided ordering anything that had meat as she had heard that millions of dogs were slaughtered annually in Cambodia and that there were more than 100 dog meat restaurants in Phnom Penh.

"Well then, tell me about yourself," John said, settling deeply in his seat.

Jessie thought it sounded like one of the questions asked in interviews. She willingly opened her heart to him - *kufungua roho,* as it was commonly referred to in Swahili. Jessie patiently explained to him about her family back home, her parents, siblings, upbringing, school and even shared her career ambitions. However, John's thirst was not easily quenched.

"So, other than vacationing and jewellery, what are your other interests?" There was a twinkle in his puppy brown eyes as he spoke.

"Hmmmm…..never really thought about that," she retorted. "I'm a huge fan of water sports." His eyes widened.

"You looked shocked. Is it because I am a woman?"

"On the contrary, I find that quite impressive. I actually have my own speed boat business."

"Are you serious?"

"Yes, I'm quite a fan myself," he said.

After that, the two chatted non-stop. Neither noticed the time slipping by. The conversation flowed like an endless river meandering around majestic scenery, topic after topic.

It felt as if they had known each other forever. Even the lapses of silence seemed entertaining. They talked about anything and everything, from politics to current social trends. John shared his constant ruminations about the plight of street children, his face darkening as he talked. Jessie sensed there was more to it but did not pry.

The waiter, who had made two polite but unsuccessful attempts to ask the pair whether they were ready to eat, beamed with joy when John finally called him and instructed him to bring the food.

Jessie shrieked when his plate was brought. The few customers in the restaurant looked unfazed.

John placed a reassuring hand on Jessie's arm.

"Pole. Please don't be scared. It's one of the popular dishes in this country.

"What! Tarantula is a delicacy?"

"Where's your sense of adventure?" John looked bemused.

By now, Jessie was beginning to calm down. The waiter reassured her that everything was all right and confirmed that Tarantulas were not poisonous.

He brought Jessie's order, another popular Cambodian dish known as amok trey, a kind of catfish steamed in a savoury coconut-based curry. The waiter also brought more sugarcane juice and invited them to enjoy their meal in Khmer, the Cambodian language.

After their meal, John settled the bill and left a handsome tip for the charming waiter.

They strolled to a waiting taxi.

"We must do this again soon," John remarked as he dropped Jessie off at her hotel. She smiled and said goodbye to him.

Once she was back in her room, she wandered back to her conversation with John. She clearly liked the man, but then again, she had only met him twice in her life and still did not know how he had found her at the mall. She pondered over his easy-going nature, his fresh persona, the aura of confidence and most importantly, his winning smile.

"I can't wait to tell Beth all about the date," Jessie thought.

She shook off her delicate sandals and had a quick change of clothes. She unlatched the necklace on her neck and removed its matching earrings. The jewellery sparkled on the dark, oak dressing table. Her admiring gaze darkened as she wondered why he had taken the trouble to buy her such an expensive gift. Moreover, jewellery of all things. She had read somewhere that when men gave you jewellery, it was often a symbol of a spark of romance, waiting to be kindled into blazing fires.

"But I can't marry the man," she mused. *"I have just met him twice and for heaven's sake, who knows what he is up to anyway?"* Nevertheless, she found herself wandering into a world of fantasy with John. An image of their family, including a beautiful daughter complete with a white picket fence, floated around in her head. Jessie quickly shook herself back to reality. Just then, the phone rang. It was Beth, wondering whether or not she was ever going to make it downstairs for an evening of fun. The hotel had theme nights during the week. This particular evening had promised an unforgettable 'African night'. Several guests from different parts of Africa were looking forward to it. Jessie was among them.

She turned off the light in her room and headed downstairs to join other revellers. She easily found Beth, who looked stunning in a

Ghanaian kente, a purely hand-woven fabric from the Ashanti people of Ghana and a royal and sacred cloth worn only in times of extreme importance. It was the cloth of kings.

"You look amazing," Jessie complimented her newly found friend. "Where did you get the kente?"

"I visited a friend in Ghana a few years back," Beth told her. She proceeded to share the details of the country with Jessie. Ghana was Africa's second-largest gold producer, previously known as the Gold Coast. Beth's friend lived in Kumasi, the capital city of the Ashanti region in Southern Ghana and known as a centre for the Ashanti culture. Beth had been lucky to visit Kumasi Central Market, West Africa's largest open- air market.

"Did you like the food?" Jessie asked.

"Of course! Especially the jollof rice, a rice dish, fried with tomato, onion, red pepper, garlic, ginger and seasoning spices. Tomato paste or puree is usually added to give it the red colour."

Like Jessie, Beth was quite well travelled. This was probably one of the reasons they got on so well even though they had only met a few days earlier and were from very different cultural backgrounds.

After a light dinner, they quickly joined the rhythm of the soothing lyrics of the live band that the hotel had hired to perform that particular evening. The band played an impressive array of instruments, one of which reminded Jessie of *nyatiti* from back home. There was also a huge Cambodian drum made from elephant hide.

As Jessie was engrossed in the dancing, she felt a hand pressing on her shoulder. Her whole body froze. "I had no idea you were such a lithe dancer." It was him.

"Well, err......thank you," she managed to stammer.

"I didn't expect to see you."

"......so soon." she added hastily, realising how dismissive her first comment may have sounded.

"Disappointed?" He asked.

"Hmmm no, not quite…, you know that's not what I mean. I was just surprised."

"I'm only joking. Relax Jessie," John said as he readied himself to dance.

He took her small trembling hand in his large steady one.

"May I have the honour of dancing with you?"

She nodded and felt virtually weightless as they twirled around the floor, oblivious to the crowd surrounding them. It seemed that they were the only people within the next thousand square miles or so. Beth cut her reverie short within minutes for the second time that day.

"I thought we were having a girls' night out. Why do we now have Mr. Boyfriend here, appearing from the blues?" Beth demanded.

"Boyfriend! Who said anything about him being my boyfriend?"

John looked amused at the whole scenario.

The whole situation felt like it was straight out of one of the Mills and Boon novels that Jessie used to read in high school.

"I think I need a drink," Jessie croaked. Her mouth felt dry.

For the second time that day, her tongue was glued to the roof of her mouth. She found herself wondering about the expression 'have you lost your tongue?' and she started to giggle.

"I didn't know I was that funny," John remarked, looking at Beth.

"She just had a long day," Beth defended her friend.

Jessie nodded. "Beth is right, John."

"I understand," he replied.

The trio danced until 11:00 pm, when Jessie politely excused herself for the evening and headed for her room. John, being the perfect gentleman he appeared to be, escorted her to the elevator after she had said goodnight to Beth.

"I had a really good night. You know what would make it even better?" "What?" Jessie asked.

"Could I have your phone number?" John asked

"Sure."

After exchanging numbers, they bade each other good night. Back in her hotel room, Jessie tossed and turned. Thoughts of John could not permit her to tumble into dreamland. The way he had looked at her with those gentle eyes of his. The way they held her and refused to let her go. The teasing curve of his lips disarmed her. His speech was melodious; she was left in a trance as she listened, lost in his carefully crafted words. Finally, Jessie fell asleep in the wee hours of the morning.

The beautiful orange rays of the sun woke her up to another day of adventure. However, she was not in a hurry; a long warm bath left her relaxed and in the mood for more action.

She took her time to prepare herself, had a warm bath, applied some makeup, and chose some casual shorts and sports shoes in readiness for a nature walk later that day.

She spotted her friend Beth seated at the far end of the dining at the breakfast table. After selecting some of the delicacies on the buffet table, she headed in Beth's direction.

"Hi Beth, good morning! Can I join you for breakfast," Jessie inquired. "Sure, welcome. You don't have to ask," Beth said with a wide smile.

"Thanks," Jessie said as she pulled a seat on the opposite side of the table.

"Tell me about your newly-found friend," Beth started with a chuckle.

"Hhmm, well, he seems nice." Jessie looked down at her food, refusing to say more.

"So how are you today?" she asked Beth, who looked a bit disappointed at Jessie's sudden change of topic.

"I'm looking forward to the nature walk. I can't wait to finally enjoy some peace and quiet at the trails and finally breathe in unpolluted air," Beth said.

After breakfast, some of the other hotel residents who were part of the Scuba diving group joined the pair.

The hotel driver drove the group to Koh Dach, one of the nature trails outside Phnom Penh. They then took a ferry ride and were there in no time. Okonkwo, one of the revellers they had met in the diving expedition, had also joined them and infused his lively sense of humour into the group. Jessie asked him if he had any connection to the character in a Nigerian book she had read in her earlier years in school. He shook his head aggressively as everyone laughed, remembering how dramatic the character in the book had been. Next, they explored a beautiful forest that even had a waterfall. Finally, the team returned to their hotel satisfied, even though they were dragging their feet.

Jessie's phone rang right on cue as she entered her room. It was John.

"Hi. How was your day?" his voice warmed her up inside.

He told her that his trip had been unfortunately cut short by a call from back home in Kenya. He requested one last meeting with Jessie before he could fly back home. John prepared her well for the occasion: a bike tour. She was to dress accordingly, and he would hire some bicycles. It had been ages since Jessie rode a bike, but she obliged because her sense of adventure was not over yet, until the holiday ended.

They met the next day at her hotel. The hotel provided transport for both of them up to the bike rental venue. They practised a bit for the sake of Jessie and signed some paperwork as a disclaimer that the company would not in any way be liable should there be any incident or accident. Jessie was already envisioning some interesting incidents, as she was already wobbling on her bike before they even left. However, she built up confidence and off they went. The Cambodian trails were quite challenging, but a breath-taking waterfall was revealed when they finally broke through the trees. They sat and had their lunch there. They visited the Tuol Sieng Genocide Museum (S-21 prison) and the killing fields of Choeung Ek. The prison is an important part of Phnom Penh's bloody history under the Khmer Rouge regime. It stands as a monument to the thousands murdered and imprisoned, while the killing fields finally stand as peaceful grounds. The experience was similarly haunting to that of the Kigali Memorial in Rwanda. While the powerful experience was very moving, it helped John and Jessie understand the culture of the Cambodian people and see how they have remained resilient and strong despite of a troubled past.

It has been said that adrenaline and sharing of touching experiences are some of the ways of forming bonds between members of the opposite sex. John had used both. They worked like a charm. Jessie could neither get the day's encounters off her mind that night nor could she stop thinking of John. He called her from the airport to say goodbye. They had a light discussion about his plans once back home in Kenya. He ended the conversation by assuring her that he was confident they would meet again in their beloved motherland, Kenya.

C H A P T E R 4

Once on the plane, John began to think about his newly found friend. A flurry of thoughts about his past equally began to assault his mind.

The year was 1996. After completing high school, John was sent to live with his uncle in Mombasa. One evening in his uncle's house, he heard an incessant pounding on his door and then the door flew open. His goliath of an uncle stood before him.

''John!'' He thundered.

''Yyyyees uncle Maina?'' he said, freezing like a cornered mouse.

''Kuja hapa!'' his uncle ordered.

John timidly followed his uncle to the garage. He demanded to know what happened, pointing to the bonnet of his beloved Datsun 1200. The alleged 'beloved' Datsun was a weatherbeaten piece of metal, most of its mustard colour faded. Whenever the ignition was switched on, the engine sputtered violently. Uncle Maina usually ended up asking John to help him push the car so he could jump - start it.

He found his uncle hovering over the bonnet of his beloved car in utter shock and disbelief. John had never seen his uncle that upset; rivulets of sweat were pouring down his fat face even though it was only 8:00 am. He wiped his brow with the back of his hand.

'"Nini ilifanyika?"

As John recounted what had happened, he slowly inched away while his uncle got closer. His uncle was breathing like a buffalo - *'mbogo nduiki'* 1

When John finished recounting how he had rammed into a tree, his uncle leaned forward, looked him in the eyes and told him to leave.

"I don't want to see you here again. Pack your things and never come back again." Those were his uncle's last words to him.

John tossed in a Bob Marley t-shirt, a pair of old faded blue jeans, some shirts, two rolls of bhang and a two-hundred-shilling note. He then stuffed his Nokia 3310 and an original leather wallet that he had pickpocketed from a man on the ferry.

He had no idea where to go, but he confidently stepped out, hailed a tuktuk and instructed the driver to drive to Jomo Kenyatta beach. John often frequented this beach on weekends to smoke marijuana with beach boys.

John spent that morning listening to the musical ocean. The turquoise sea stretched endlessly before him. The sky was a rich hue of light blue expanse, with white fluffy cotton balls floating in it.

He was desperately trying to forget the ugly scene with his uncle. However, his bulldog face remained etched in John's mind. Tears ebbed slowly down his face. John had not intended to hurt his dear uncle Maina.

Now, he was homeless. The pent-up dam opened, and the tears resumed. He forlornly recalled the beginning of his life as an orphan, the dejection of losing his mother at an early age, and the feeling of being unwanted after his father abandoned him.

When his father later died, John did not quite know what to feel. His body was numb, with not even a twinge of sadness in his heart as he reminisced on their last moments together. His father had his back turned to him, bent over the kitchen sink, rinsing out the last cup he would ever use. When he finished, John's father spoke the last words to his son and left, never to be seen alive again, "So long John." John's father died in a horrific car crash.

In the state of being deluded, he pictured his uncle and started sobbing again.

A growl in his stomach told him that it was already lunchtime. John stopped crying and reluctantly got up to try and see where he could get something to eat. A tall figure blocked his path. Looming shadows immediately surrounded him. Fear gripped John as he tried looking around for a way to escape. The shadows edged closer until he could smell their breaths, pungent with alcohol. The tall one asked if he fancied a boat ride on one of the speedboats. When John told them he had very little money, they laughed until tears streamed down their cheeks.

"Sonko kama wewe huna hela?"

The young men looked incredulous at John as he insisted that he had no money to spend, narrating to them everything that had happened since the previous night up to his exile that morning. They nodded with empathy and asked how they could help. John told them he needed a place to sleep. They burst into laughter again when he told them he had never slept on the streets before. They promised to show him the ropes of this new life.

John's new friends invited him to play a game of poker, where he, unfortunately, lost all his money to the conniving beach boys. They told him to come back the following day, and they would introduce him to someone. One of the more mature boys in the group, Mwangangi, offered John his phone number, which he accepted. Mwangangi then shoved a handful of cassava crisps and madafu into John's hands. That was, of course, by no means a meal of the caliber John was used to at his uncle's house, but he had no choice. They left him standing there, open-mouthed.

John spent the remaining part of the day looking for a suitable place to lay his head. He felt lucky that he had a stolen blanket from the bed he had lain on at Uncle Maina's house for the past one and half years, as the nights in the coastal region could get chilly, especially towards the wee hours of the morning.

Finally, he spotted a veranda on an abandoned street. The cement felt cold on his body as he huddled against the wall, his thin blanket barely protecting him from the cutting wind.

It was 6:00 pm. It was getting dark. John carefully unfolded his Bob Marley t-shirt and some shorts and changed into them. He then remembered he had a packet of half-eaten peanuts. He munched them in two mouthfuls. Afterwards, he used a stone as a pillow, with his rucksack on top, and settled in. It now dawned upon John that his life had hit rock bottom.

The day's events replayed in John's mind as he slept, but with nightmarish variations. His fat uncle was sitting on him at one time, squashing him, and his guts were spilling out. John woke up screaming, experiencing terrible pain from his rear end. He started jumping up and down, but the creature would not let him go. John tried to feel the back of his shorts with his left hand. The thing bit his fingers, and he screamed again. John started groping in the dark, trying to find his phone. Instead, stepping on another crab and realised, to his dismay that the entire veranda was full of them. It was like a scene straight out of a horror movie.

The pain from the butt-biting crab on his behind was getting unbearable. He yanked the stubborn creature that had inflicted so much suffering off his body in one swift motion. He winced as an almost electric wave rippled through his body. He had to get out of this living hell. He backtracked his steps to where his backpack was and managed to find his Nokia 3310. Using its flashlight to see, he threw the few things lying on the floor into the backpack and left the veranda. He figured he could make it if he could tread carefully amidst the crawling crustaceans. This he miraculously did and heaved a sigh of relief as he breathed in the fresh air.

He checked his phone and saw that it was 3:30 am, approximately thirty minutes after the attack. He had no idea where to go at that time of the morning. He knew that he did not want another crab encounter, so John walked as far away as he could from his initial home of horrors, even though his backside was killing him.

Years later, John's life completely turned around. He managed to set up a successful boat business courtesy of his street friends, to the extent that he could fly out of the country for business meetings.

This turn in fortune brought him to his current state of meeting someone like Jessie, who showed promise to be something more in his life.

CHAPTER 5

After coming back to Kenya, Jessie started seeing John. She had dated before, but it had never been like this. When John held her, it felt right. She let her body sag and her muscles become loose. He gave her the respect of an equal but cradled her like a cherished child. In that embrace, she felt her worries lose their keen sting and her optimism raise its head from the dirt.

John's stoic soul brought serenity to her own. He allowed her to be herself; she felt more comfortable around him than any other person. Their conversations were genuine, their spark undeniable. It always seemed like time was never on their side when they were together; they became more and more hungry for each other's company.

"Sweetheart, if I am with a group of my best friends and you're not there, then I'm alone," John confided in her.

John was certainly not perfect, but he made Jessie feel protected as if he was her guardian angel. The couple developed mutual trust, sharing intimate intricacies after a long workday. They rode through every storm together, waiting to see what the new dawn would bring.

* * * * *

One evening after work, John called Jessie. "Jessie, I keep thinking about you. Next week seems too long of a period to wait to see you," he confessed.

John was aware that he probably sounded like a love-struck high school kid, but he was out of control by now. He also knew it was time to let the cat out of the bag.

John arrived in Nairobi from Mombasa the following Wednesday. He was promptly outside Jessie's apartment in Westlands by ten in the morning. Westlands was a busy but nice suburban, in the up-market part of the city. It was once serene, but it was now overcrowded due to the increasing population and skyrise commercial buildings. Westlands did have a positive side to it, however. It was an all-in-one stop area which meant that one could find all necessary amenities. It even had a post office. There was no need to go to the central business district in Nairobi city.

The pair took a taxi to a popular coffee shop in one of the malls. They found a quiet spot on the outdoor balcony and settled in. She carefully arranged her turquoise kitenge dress as she sat. John examined his date. Jessie did not even wear any makeup! He concluded that she did not need it. Her innocent eyes were endearing. If the eyes are the gateway to the soul, the lips are the same thing for the body. He felt that Jessie's lips held a promise of passion and the sweetness to come.

He studied the rest of her, noticing how the deep box pleats of her dress accentuated her waist.

"My mother would be very impressed to see you looking like that," he commented.

Jessie lowered her eyes to the floor.

They ordered coffee and spring rolls. The two weeks since John's last business trip felt like centuries. It was difficult to hide how much he had missed her. The sun streaked in, creating a lazy, relaxed mood as John updated her about how his boat business was doing. It was the peak season for tourism, being the month of December. Many tourists from Europe and America had come to escape the harsh winter and enjoy the lovely weather in Kenya.

Likewise, Jessie shared how numerous weddings in that month made her experience a boom in her business. The majority of brides preferred to have kitenge outfits in their bridal parties. She also told him funny stories about the rest of her holiday in Cambodia.

John stretched out his long legs and straightened his khaki pants. He rubbed his large nose, a habit he had developed lately when around Jessie.

John began to narrate his past life to her, pouring out his soul. He explained to Jessie how he had moved from home to home, bounced like a tennis ball; rejection seemed to ooze out of his skin. He had entreated God repeatedly, why he had not died in his mother's womb. He revealed to Jessie that the straw that finally broke the camel's back was the incident with his uncle in Mombasa. John had managed to live with him for two years before all hell broke loose, and he found himself in the loneliness of the streets of Mombasa.

John's voice grew more profound. He leaned in towards her and spoke in a low tone. "Jessie, I know we have been friends for a while now. I don't want us to have a 'situationship' if you know what I mean," he said.

"I know exactly what you mean. I don't want us to find ourselves in that scenario either where it is a friendship with all the perks associated with relationships, except it's not defined, yet we spend a lot of time together but we can't refer to each other as boyfriend or girlfriend," Jessie replied, allowing a flicker of a smile to cross her lips.

"Great! We're on the same page," John said, smiling "You are beautiful Jessie. Outside and inside. I want to know all about you…I would like to spend more time with you - exclusively. Jessie, we have not really discussed this plainly but I was wondering if this would be a problem to someone else."

"Well, what do you mean by this?" Jessie feigned ignorance though she knew exactly what he was talking about.

"Jessie, ever since we met in Cambodia, I have not been able to keep my mind off you. You enamour me with your smile, your essence, your presence. I…. I w-w-w-would like you to be my girlfriend. What do you think about that?"

"I need some time to think things through," Jessie responded, looking anywhere but at John.

"No worries my dear. We can continue this conversation another time," John replied.

He signalled to the waiter to come and then paid the bill. The taxi he had ordered to pick up Jessie arrived. He accompanied her back to her apartment. Before she got out of the car, he held her hand slightly longer, his dark eyes boring into hers.

"I really love your company. That makes it really hard for me to say goodbye," John said with sincerity.

Jessie smiled and gently withdrew her hand.

"I have to go, John",

The urgency in her voice made John hurriedly step out and open the car door for Jessie.

"Good night John." She quickly stepped into her house.

* * * * *

Once inside, Jessie changed into comfortable shorts and a t-shirt. Finally, she had time to herself to ponder the situation. Jessie had been in previous relationships but had never imagined she could feel this deeply about a man. As this was what it had come down to, she had to control these crazy feelings and somehow go back to her former self; a calm, controlled, and poised Jessie, with a witty answer and always ready to respond to any challenging question life threw at her.

However, she could not honestly answer the question: was she ready for love? The response to this question would have further consequences. It was like the concept of a decision tree which she had learned about in school. The teacher wrote a question on the blackboard. The class answered, and more arrows were drawn below the answer. If yes, there was a consequence. If no, another arrow was drawn. The exercise had seemed so long that the blackboard was full by the time they were done.

Jessie analysed her current situation; if yes, indeed she was ready for love, was she willing to settle down – marry this man and bear his children? To spend the remainder of her years soiling her delicate hands doing odd house chores to complement the house help? To clear sinks full of dishes every night after a long day? To have her beautiful trim body blow up to accommodate other human beings growing inside her iron board tummy? Most importantly, was she ready to surrender her personal space and be accountable to another human being other than her parents – especially about her every movement and decision?

These were several questions that ensued from the initial one. They required deep thought and inner reflection. Jessie was going to do exactly that. She needed time to think about the response to his question as it had only been two months since their initial meeting in Cambodia. However, a certain inner peace told her that this man was 'the one'.

Two weeks later, they were on a long phone call.

"I've been doing a lot of thinking about the question you asked me about"

"And….?" John queried.

"I wouldn't mind spending more time with you, John."

"As my boyfriend," she added.

Ever since John and Jessie had officially agreed they were dating, they had grown much closer, candidly sharing things that they never did before. Six months later, John arrived early one morning on the train from Mombasa. He offered to take Jessie shopping at Kangemi market. She preferred to do her grocery shopping in the local market, where she had established relationships with the sellers of fresh produce. John got into the car and drove Jessie to the market in her silver Mercedes. They arrived exactly ten minutes later, parked the car at an adjacent fuel station, and casually walked into the market.

Within an hour, glimpses of the first glowing of the Nairobi sky would begin to show; the market would quickly fill with chicken, vegetables and hundreds of people with all kinds of wares to sell.

As usual, Kangemi was full of hustle and bustle. Mamas trading stories animatedly. Young men selling potatoes and young women excitedly calling out to customers to buy their fresh *nyanyas* and *vitunguus*. Jessie recognized one of them.

"*Mambo* Jessie!" she greeted Jessie in Sheng.

"*Poa sana* Mama Nyambu," Jessie responded in Sheng as well.

"*Sema nikuuzie?*" she gazed inquiringly at Jessie.

Jessie told her the items she needed while John helped pack them in bags. Finally, they said goodbye and visited a few more stalls before leaving the market.

After shopping, Jessie and John went home and began to sort out the groceries they had bought. While in the kitchen, in the middle of washing the vegetables, John stopped and looked Jessie in the eye. As he towered over her, she sensed he was about to divulge something life-changing.

"Jessie, with you, even the mundane things in life like washing vegetables are fun. I want to do this forever with you. Will you be my wife?" He asked, gazing imploringly into her eyes.

Jessie hesitated. She had grown to love John dearly. She was quiet for a long time.

"Yes!" Jessie finally replied.

"I promise I will make you a very happy woman." John assured Jessie, giving her a big hug, that smile she loved gracing his face.

Jessie did not doubt then that she had made the right decision in her heart.

Something struck her about the proposal she had just accepted. Where was the ring? She wondered. John was not a stingy man, so that could not have been the issue. She, however hid her disappointment and decided to go with the flow.

Later that evening, John took her out for a quiet dinner. He excused himself to go to the restroom, which she found odd as they had just left the house. A group of waiters surrounded her in a few minutes, and started singing, "*Malaika, nakupenda. Malaika.*" John's deep voice joined them from the back. He was carrying a gorgeous bouquet of flowers.

"For you my love," he said, reaching forward to give them to her as he pecked her lightly on the cheek.

Jessie blushed involuntarily and accepted the flowers. The waiter quickly put them in a vase for her. John was looking breathtakingly handsome in his tuxedo, and it was a struggle to take her eyes off him.

"Soup?" he inquired of her.

"Please," she said.

He ordered two bowls of mushroom soup and some bread rolls. They had fish with an accompaniment of roast potatoes for the main course. After eating, the waiter brought the bill and thrust it next to her in a brown leather holder. Jessie was now beginning to think her fears of John being a miser had been confirmed. She had no problems splitting bills or even treating him, but she felt this was supposed to be a romantic dinner. Besides, it was his initiative to take her out. When a person offered to take another out, the initiator usually paid the entire bill in their setting. Otherwise, the invited party could end up getting a rude shock and may not even have been financially prepared.

Jessie again decided to play it cool and instead took out the bill. As she did so, something fell out of the holder. She stared in amazement as she held it up to the light. The singing waiters drew closer once more, playing a soothing, slow tune. The music got louder and more flowers appeared on their table. John got out of his chair and walked over to her; he slipped the shiny diamond ring onto her slim middle finger on her left hand. The ring's band measured 4 ½ cm, and the diamond was a .73 Ct diamond measuring 5.91x5.87x3.5mm. The full bezel on the ring protected the diamond and gave the impression that the diamond was much larger than it was.

It was simple, elegant, and stunning.

After John paid the bill, the couple left the restaurant beaming with joy. Unfortunately, John had to take a flight back to Mombasa that night. This time Jessie escorted him to the airport in her car. She held her fiancé tightly and only released him when she heard his flight announcement.

C H A P T E R 6

One day, while John and Jessie were strolling down Kimathi Street in Nairobi window shopping, they bumped into someone unlikely. It was Malkia, Jessie's small sister.

"What are you doing in Nairobi?" Jessie asked, shocked.

"Am I confined to spend the rest of my life in that sweaty town?" Malkia responded, half-teasing. She adored Mombasa.

"Oh, Malkia, this is my fiancé, John." Jessie pointed to John, smiling apologetically at John, her eyes begging forgiveness for momentarily forgetting him. "Sweets, this is my younger sister Malkia".

John beamed and gripped Malkia hand, firmly shaking it. "It's such a pleasure to meet you, I've heard so much about you," he said.

"I hope my sister hasn't been telling you about all those embarrassing incidents I had in my adventurous childhood," Malkia remarked, looking accusingly at her sister.

"I've heard nothing but good things about you." John reassured her.

"Is that so? Jess is such a darling..."

"We should organise a double date one of these days, now that we are going to be family," Jessie jumped in hearing the sarcasm in her sister's response.

"That would be wonderful," Malkia responded, uninterested.

They settled on dinner at a popular hotel in town the following week.

* * * * *

It was Friday evening. The double date night was finally here. The setting was very romantic, with soft music and candles all around. One could scarcely see or hear the madness of the Nairobi traffic or the loud music from the bars that lined Kimathi Street. Jessie and John arrived first. They ordered some white wine as they waited for Malkia and her date to arrive. They were half an hour late. Heads turned to look at them as they made their grand entrance. Malkia was dressed in a very low cut, blue dress with a string of pearl earrings and a matching necklace. Her dress was very short and left little to the imagination. Her date was about her height with long, unkempt dreadlocks and a shifty look about him. One did not have to be a professional matchmaker to see that this was definitely not a match made in heaven. The pair quickly found the table Jessie and John had reserved for them. Jessie stood up to hug her sister as John stretched out his hand in a hearty handshake, which Malkia's date returned amicably. Malkia on the other hand lingered, holding John's hand longer than necessary. He gently withdrew it as he invited them to sit. They decided to order coastal cuisine. The chicken biryani was mouthwatering. After they had finished, Malkia excused herself to visit the washroom. She took a long time. When she came back, she had an extra shade of her bright red lipstick. Before taking her place at the table, she brushed gently against John. He did not notice anything unusual about this, as the alcohol crept into his brain, nor did the rest. They ordered more white wine and everyone was in a mellow mood. Someone commented about the recently implemented 'alcoblow' system, which was meant to detect drivers under a certain level of alcoholic influence, and how they could potentially all be spending the night in a slightly different place than the nice hotel they were in; a place like the Central police station. They all laughed at this. Malkia smiled coyly at John, stretched out her foot and tapped his lightly under the table. This time, despite the wine, he noticed and looked surprised. He glanced at his fiancée who was sitting by his side and seemed to be on cloud nine, as she poured more wine. At last, dinner was over and goodbyes were said. When no one was looking, Malkia slipped a piece of paper into John's trouser pocket. He found it later in the privacy of his bedroom. It had her number and an invitation to meet her at a famous hotel in the city centre, the following night, alone. Malkia, was certainly not showing any trait of loyalty despite her name suggesting that, John thought. He had made up his mind to tell Jessie but then thought the better of it. This would just cause tension between them and from some of Jessie's childhood stories, he figured their relationship had never been smooth sailing. However, he decided he would meet up with Malkia and find out exactly what Malkia wanted from him, although he already had a clue.

Jessie was working late the following night; hence John did not have to make up an excuse regarding his whereabouts that evening. He took a taxi to the hotel Malkia had mentioned. He told the staff at the lobby that he was expected at room 1960. He planned how he was going to put Malkia off. He was getting married for crying out loud. And not to just anyone, but her own flesh and blood sister.

Malkia was dressed in an even lower cut top – if that was even possible – than the previous night. John knew right away that he should have left, right there and then as the scent of the expensive perfume she had doused herself in, wafted from the room. Yet his feet refused to budge as he stared at her. He felt very much like Joseph in the Bible, who found himself facing a similar temptation from Potiphar's wife. Gathering some inner strength, he did not know he possessed, John started to turn back the way he had come but Malkia grabbed his hand and pulled him into the room.

"Jessie will be working late today. I confirmed," she assured him.

John was appalled by Malkia's unabashed lack of integrity but when she moved closer, hugging him tight, she offered little to no resistance. She was all over him in seconds. Little by little, John found himself breaking the promise of love, commitment and devotion that he had made when he offered the beautiful engagement ring to Jessie. He had compromised and offered his body to another, other than the love of his life.

It was four hours later when John finally emerged from room 1960 and took a taxi back to Jessie's place. Pangs of guilt crowded his mind. John felt as though he could never face Jessie again. However, he had to. He was getting married to the woman of his dreams, he reminded himself.

The next day Jessie had a sunny smile on her face that matched the flowery sundress she was wearing. She threw her arms around him and hugged him hard.

"Honey, sorry about last night. Work was crazy, but now I'm all yours," she said this with a knowing, cheeky look on her face.

John tried to hide his dismay as she kissed him. Jessie noticed his sudden change in behaviour and drew back.

"What's wrong, hun?" She asked her big, round eyes clouding over with concern.

"Nothing, my love, I'm just a little bit tired," he replied.

"Why, you weren't working last night like me, you know," Jessie teased. "I'm the only one allowed to be tired or have a 'headache'.

"I know, I know, please let's just relax today, cuddle and watch a great movie I selected just for you."

"If you say so, dear," Jessie conceded defeat, but thought he was acting a little strange.

 John's cell phone rang as Jessie was in the kitchen.

"Hello handsome," purred the voice on the other end.

"How did you get my number?" He hissed into the phone. He had used his office line to call her the previous day.

"Come on, that's easy, you're my relative!" Malkia pretended to be hurt by this question.

"What do you want?" John asked angrily.

"I just thought I'd say hello and ask if you would be free to meet up tonight."

"No I'm not, and don't call me again unless it's life-threatening."

"But it is," she insisted.

 John had had enough and disconnected the phone.

"Who was that dear?" Jessie's sing-song voice floated from the kitchen.

"Just some people from work, love," he lied, feeling sick about it.

"I hope they don't want to make you work on a Saturday."

"Nothing like that my dear," John said, knowing only too well, how true this statement actually was.

She emerged soon after with some golden brown delicious looking chapatis, minced meat stew and salad on the side.

"Mmmm, this is the main reason I am marrying you," John teased, circling her waist with his arm.

"I thought that love had something to do with it," Jessie retorted playfully as she set down the tray of food.

 John immediately switched off his phone. He had had enough drama for the day.

John continued to see Malkia secretly during the next couple of weeks leading to the wedding despite his guilt eating away at him every time he met his fiancée. It was as though she had bewitched him. Jessie had noticed how distracted he had become of late and every time he would say, it was pressure from work and planning the wedding. However, John had the uncomfortable feeling that she would one day find out. The Swahili saying, *siku za mwizi ni arobaini* would finally hold water.

* * * * *

Malkia, on the other hand, felt absolutely no remorse. She was getting even for all those childhood days when Jessie had made her feel insignificant. The day Jessie had introduced John to her she knew it was time. John was going to be instrumental in her plan. She began to feel the fits of rage she had experienced all her life forming knots in her stomach.

Each time they met during the wedding arrangements, Malkia secretly gloated over her conquest, at Jessie's ignorant bliss and at the clever way she had managed to keep the whole affair secret.

Malkia had been diagnosed with bipolar disorder shortly after completing high school. Her mood swings were irritating, especially to those closest to her. She had been an emotional wreck, one moment on a euphoric high – happy and at peace with the world; the next moment, down with depression. She was still battling with her condition; her emotional highs came from being around John and getting her revenge on Jessie. She saw no reason to end the illicit relationship.

* * * * *

For John on the other hand, he felt that the entire situation was getting stickier by the day. What if Malkia got pregnant? How would she explain the baby's photocopy resemblance to John? Besides, Malkia had lately been acting weird, all pumped up with self-confidence whose source only John knew too well. Jessie noticed this, during a visit to Malkia's house with John one day.

"Seems like her majesty's been walking on air these days," Jessie teased.

"My boyfriend's been treating me extremely well lately," Malkia quipped.

"Oh, that's nice! If only mine here could catch on," Jessie pinched John's arm playfully.

He shot a nasty glance at Malkia.

"Jessie darling, please, don't we have some shopping to do?" John implored, his eyes softening, desperate.

"Shopping!" She looked incredulous. "I thought you hated it!" "I do honey, but this time, I needed to pick up a tool for the car, from the supermarket."

"Okay then. Let's catch up another time. I guess *mzee amechoka,*" she winked at Malkia, who threw back her head and laughed maniacally.

"Sweets, you looked upset back there," Jessie later commented.

John had not even noticed his clenched fists. He would have liked to strangle Malkia right there and then at her house, only that her sister may not have been so keen to marry him after this. His heart was still pounding furiously, as if it wanted to fly right out of his chest that very minute. *Perhaps that wouldn't be so bad,* he mused. *Put me out of my misery.* Oh *Jess, what am I doing to you, to us,* he thought.

John felt trapped in a bottomless pit where he sank deeper and deeper into the black abyss. He could not end his relationship with Malkia. She was like a magnet. He simply could not resist her.

C H A P T E R 7

A marriage is a deep and loving friendship, one in which the love is so strong that each would sacrifice for the other. Jessie and John were already learning this even during their wedding preparations.

The days that followed were filled with numerous planning discussions; the task of intertwining two cultures that were completely different, while ensuring minimal friction between the two families was a herculean task.

According to cultural expectations in Kenya, the young man needed to inform his girlfriend's parents of his intent to marry her. Dowry payment was to precede the wedding. Specifically in John's tribe, which was the Gikuyu, there was a series of events to be undertaken.

The first one was *kumenya mucii* which involved getting to know the bride's home. The second in the series of events was *kŭhanda ithige*, which literally means planting a branch of a tree. The third one is *kúracia* which is the actual dowry/bride price payment. This process lasts a lifetime in this community; *"Rúracio rútithiraga"* is the direct translation in Kikuyu.

The next one is *Itara*, getting to see the nest or nesting place of their daughter, which is a visit to the groom's homestead.

The final event is *Kúguraria* also known as *gútinia kiande*, the traditional kikuyu wedding.

John was happy about how he had moved things along by finally proposing to the love of his life.

He and Jessie made plans for the initial visit to her parents in order to set the date of the wedding after obtaining their consent. John was accompanied by his childhood friends and business associates. The driveway that led to their home in an estate called Kitusuru was never ending. The aura was stunning. Tall Moringa trees formed an overarching canopy over the driveway. Climbing plants, roses and oriental lilies grew alongside it, creating an oasis of calm in the madness of Nairobi. It was like being in a botanical garden on either side, of which in fact they were, as they later found out from Jessie's mum who was a botanist. When they finally arrived, Jessie's mother met them at the door, and ushered them into a lobby.

''Welcome to our humble abode. Please wait here and we will be with you shortly,'', she said.

Though she seemed sincere and warm, there was nothing humble about the posh house. John remembered that Jessie told him her father had gifted her a BMW on her eighteenth birthday. He could see how credible that was if this was the kind of home she was brought up in. The other friends were impressed too.

Mwangangi, who had been tongue tied up to this point, a rare feat for him, whistled in amazement.

"Si umeangukia bro," he exclaimed.

"Lakini hela sio za Jessi," John protested.

Another of his friends pointed out that family money was exactly that – family money.

Jessie's father Mr. Omwando surfaced from the blue. The young men were startled, especially John and Mwangangi.

"Why are you people so late?" Mr. Omwando asked.

He was barricading the door and looked like he was not going to move an inch until he had his answers. He glared at John and Mwangangi's dreadlocks. Mrs. Omwando came to the rescue. "John, our daughter's fiancé, had communicated that he and his friends had been delayed unexpectedly," she said, pointing to John. "I haven't met the others but I believe they shall introduce themselves once we are seated" Mr. Omwando was still scanning the young men condescendingly, beneath his spectacles which were delicately balancing on his wide nose. He reluctantly moved aside as Jessie's mother quickly ushered them in, apologising for the hold up even though it had clearly been her husband's fault.

They sat down on a plush sofa in the middle of the living room. Beautifully upholstered armrests complemented its impeccably done tailoring.

A woollen rug caressed their bare feet; in this context, it is considered extremely rude to the host if the visitors enter with shoes.

Jessie's father formally introduced himself as the head of the home. He told them that he was a surgeon by profession. John imagined Mr. Omwando chasing him and his pals round the room with a scalpel. He almost laughed at this but a stern look from Mr. Omwando quickly stifled any outward display of mirth. Mr. Omwando assured them that he had not been born with a silver spoon in his mouth; he believed in hard work as a pathway to success. He further confided that he was not impressed by the spineless, spoiled young men he saw around nowadays, squandering their parents' wealth. He was scrutinising John and his friends, in a manner insinuating that he did not think they were any different from this pathetic lot. John was waiting for the opportunity to defend himself and his cronies. He jumped eagerly at the chance as soon as Mr. Omwando indicated he could speak.

And so John spoke. "Like you sir, neither I, nor any of these young men were born into wealthy families."

He paused, wondering since when that was a crime. He knew several friends who had been born into money. Their parents had taught them the principles of hard work. These resulted to the making of serious entrepreneurs.

"I struggled to build my boat business." He narrated the ordeal of competing with other established boat businesses at the coast, most of whom were natives, whereas he was simply a '*mtu wa bara*' or someone from the mainland.

By the time he was done speaking, Mr. Omwando looked visibly moved and so did his wife as well as John's friends, even though they had heard this story before.

"That was very courageous of you," Mr. Omwando commented.

"Thank you, sir," John, replied.

Mr. Omwando leaned forward in his seat, looking intently into John's eyes.

"Look. You seem like a reasonable young man or else my usually levelheaded Jessie would not have fallen for you." He then threw his head back and laughed, as if he had just told the funniest joke in the world.

John and his friends also joined in the laughter, though cautiously as they did not want to offend Mr. Omwando. The drama at the door had been enough.

The second visit happened two months later. It had a more mature age group than the first, making the mood more sombre. Jessie's four aunts along with their husbands were invited. John came with three uncles and two aunts from Murang'a. They arrived promptly at 2:00 pm as had been agreed. John was dressed in a kitenge shirt from Jessie's men's collection, black trousers and black leather shoes. This time, the dreadlocks were gone from his head. It had taken a lot of soul searching for John to shave the dreadlocks since they had been a part of his personality. However, they also reminded him of his dark past and yet he had moved on and was about to make a fresh start in life; this time, as somebody's husband.

Jessie had to be hidden somewhere behind the scenes, while negotiations ensued.

Meanwhile, meat was furiously boiling in two huge pots. Goat ribs simmered in the grill. The head chef effortlessly turned ugali in an oversized saucepan with his sturdy arms. It was brown ugali. John's oldest uncle, Mr. Kamau said a prayer. He asked God to guide them, quoting Psalm 32:8, "I will instruct you and teach you in the way you should go; I will guide you with My eye."

As he prayed, he felt a warning in his gut about the impending wedding. This was not the first time he had experienced communication in this way from God. When he finished praying, he knew he would have to tell his wife about the nudging feeling that would not go away. Mr. Kamau silently signalled Mr. Omwando who cleared his throat and began.

"I would like to welcome all of you who are seated here to this auspicious occasion – the coming together of two families, to impact the future of our children. I would like to make it clear that we are not here to make things difficult for our potential in-laws. It is in our best interests to see these children settle as quickly and as smoothly as possible."

With that, the negotiations began and went on for the next three hours. At last, the final bride price was agreed upon. Additionally, some gifts were requested from John's aunts – a big sufuria or saucepan, lesos or khangas- traditional cotton print fabric, tied around the waist by women. John's uncles were requested to bring five cows, two goats and a long coat called rimana.

The ladies broke into ululations. The bride-to-be was finally allowed to enter the room. Jessie greeted everyone shyly and helped to serve the food. John and his relatives left by 7:00 pm, satisfied that all had gone well.

 Or, had it?

Mr. Kamau shared what he had experienced with his wife, who suggested that they discuss the incident with the pastors who were counselling the couple, as well as John's relatives. Unfortunately, this never happened.

* * * * *

"Arirririrriiiiiiiiiii!" The sound of ululations could be heard all over the normally quiet compound of the Omwandos. It was the day of the final visit by the in-laws. John's aunts circled outside the house, dancing in jubilation. They were singing traditional Kikuyu songs, requesting to be allowed into their in-laws' house. Someone inside translated what they were singing, to which Jessie's aunts responded with songs of their own, artfully refusing to comply and instead requesting John's aunts to show what they had to offer to prove their

worthiness to be granted entry. The gifts were then presented: the khangas for the ladies, the long coat – *rimana* as well as the big *sufuria*. These items seemed to appease the in-laws and the gate was flung wide open.

More ululations and much dancing broke out.

This final visit had far more festivity. The jovial mood was definitely quite different from the sombre atmosphere in the two previous visits. A goat was slaughtered by the men. The same uncles that had accompanied John in the first visit were here. This time, his friends, including Mwangangi had also been invited. The function was in a big white tent in the Omwandos' compound. The merriment lasted until late in the night. The food was an endless river. The men at some point entered the house to present the bride price to Jessie's father and uncles. Jessie's relatives looked very happy.

The deal had been sealed. The couple could now proceed with their wedding plans.

C H A P T E R   8

Jessie could not believe that the wedding day was finally at hand. Though her mind was still absorbed in a flurry of thoughts, a wave of relief was slowly washing over her. She had mysteriously morphed from a bridezilla, ditching the drama queen antics for a minimalist approach to the wedding.

For Jessie, the more the grandeur displayed in the wedding, the less the depth attached to the union it represented; a lifetime of two souls knit together. Excessiveness would be a stark contrast to the sacrifices that the couple would make in their marriage.

Jessie preferred to keep the wedding simple.

The bridesmaids had arrived at Jessie's parents' home the previous night. There were only three of them. The reason was Jessie had very few close friends and she liked it that way.

She knew in her heart she could count on her best friends, Samantha, Wabi and Beth. Beth had actually flown all the way from America two days earlier; a real sacrifice from a forever friend. The last time they had seen each other was in Cambodia, where they first met. Wabi was her childhood best friend; they had grown up in the same neighbourhood in Kitusuru. She and Samantha had been desk mates in high school and university

On the eve of the wedding, the bride and bridesmaids stayed up late telling horror stories of perpetual slavery of wives in marriage. Fortunately, her best friend Samantha had a different view. Being happily married, she spoke with deep conviction that not all men are dogs or pigs. By midnight, Jessie had to literally force her friends to go to bed. She could not afford to have them ruin the wedding photos if they showed up with bags under their eyes due to lack of sleep. They agreed and retired into the guest wing that had been prepared for them. Jessie finally drifted off to sleep. She was acutely aware that this was her last night as a single woman.

Morning came. A huge breakfast had been served. It was a mixture of traditional dishes from both cultures. From the Kikuyu side, they had *ndumas*, and, *githeri* Jessie's mum had prepared an elaborate spread of brown ugali, accompanied by goat meat, *nsaga* and *managu*, traditional Kisii vegetables renowned for their unquestionable nutritious value. The bridal party could not afford to proceed to the wedding on empty stomachs and so they wiped out the entire spread in front of them.

After the 'wedding' breakfast, Jessie's friends helped her wear the wedding dress.

The beautician was already waiting to apply make-up on the bridal party. She started by applying a natural shade of foundation cream on Jessie's face. Then Jessie allowed her to do something she had never done in her whole life – put on her fake eyelashes. Her eyelids weighed a tonne! Her eyebrows were done next, using a natural brown eye pencil to blend with her dark skin. The beautician then applied a baby pink hue of lip gloss. Jessie was glad that her hair and nails had been done the previous day. The maids then wore their outfits in turn. They were fitting kitenge dresses from Jessie's clothing line, a vivacious blend of fuschia and shades of grey colours.

A series of ululations pierced the curtain of crisp morning air like a sharp knife, and tore it into shreds.

"So soon," Jessie thought and she started to panic.

Her mother who was standing by her side placed a reassuring hand around her daughter's shoulder.

"Everything will be okay dear" she encouraged her daughter, although she was also beginning to feel emotional.

The camera man appeared and pointed his camera towards them. He proudly explained that it took spectacular thirty-two point five megapixel images; it also captured emotions that the human eye could not notice.

"I'd like a brief interview with the bride, her mother and best maid," he finally requested.

In her interview, Jessie candidly shared her fears and apprehension of marriage. Her mother had a different source of anxiety. That of a mother whose daughter and source of pride was being whisked away by a man she had met only a few months ago.

The camera man was used to this and cajoled them into pouring out their hearts.

The interview drew to a close. More ululations sounded. It was John's aunties dancing and singing Kikuyu songs, asking to see the bride. Jessie's aunties responded with Kisii songs, in praise of the bride and emphasising on her worth. Soon everyone was singing, almost like a music festival competition until the bridal party surfaced and entered the black, land cruisers that had been waiting to whisk the bride away. The motorcade with other groups followed. They arrived promptly at the Anglican Church at 11:00am, surprisingly on time.

Several friends and relatives were already gathered at the church, an impressive building that was more than a hundred years old, located near Uhuru Park. The church was designed in ancient Gothic style and was built from Kenyan stone, which resulted in a seamless blending of the two cultures. Its interior featured ribbed ceilings and impressive arches. Stunning round stained glass windows stood proudly behind the altar.

The singing continued until the bridal party stepped out of their car. The maids got out first. Everyone admired their outfits until the bride appeared - a huge bouquet of fuchsia roses spilling from Jessie's hand. Her white wedding gown was long and flowing with layers of lace giving volume to her trim frame. Tiny silver stars hid in its folds, appearing only when she moved. A piece of Kitenge fabric had been carefully woven into the back of the dress. It was a single strip of cloth, done in a zigzag from the lower back all the way to the nape of her neck. The kitenge had exactly the same fuschia and grey hues that the bridesmaids were wearing.

The church band started to play. It was time for the bride procession to proceed into the church. The groom and his groomsmen had been waiting. One by one, each maid was received by her partner groomsman as she danced. John also had three men in his line-up; Mwangangi, his best friend, was the best man; two other friends were groomsmen. John was an only child hence the reason no siblings were in his line-up. Last but not least, Jessie and two small flower girls in polka dot dresses danced in slowly. Their circular dresses were made out of the same kitenge as the 'big girls'.

John's eyes grew moist. He never imagined his life coming together in this sort of way. It was one of those moments in movies where time stands still. John's eyes held hers, and followed her down the aisle; his brazen fixation only being broken by the sound of the band. Everyone belted out the lyrics of a popular Afro Fusion tune that the band was playing. His bride finally arrived and her parents reluctantly let go of her arms. The look on her father's face showed this was quite a struggle. After all, she had been daddy's girl all her life. John exhaled.

Jessie suddenly noticed something odd about the complete bridal party. There were three page boys and not two as originally planned. How could this be? At this point, there was nothing she could do but watch helplessly. Jessica decided not to allow this to ruin her mood- this was her day.

The reverend stepped forward and began the sermon. "God's ways are not your ways, nor His thoughts like ours!" Reverend George boomed into the microphone.

"God is a God of plan, purpose, desire, design and objectivity. He knows our end, right from the beginning. He has the blueprint of our lives in His hands. He is a God of much more. " He

paused to address the couple.

"John and Jessie, entrust God with your marriage. Make Him the centre and you will never regret it. He has much more in store for you, than you can ever imagine."

Then he addressed the whole congregation: "Love God and others. That, dear beloved of God, is a summary of God's law," he concluded.

He motioned the couple to approach the front of the cathedral. It was time to say the vows.

There was an awkward moment when Reverend George asked if there was anyone who objected to the union. John resisted the urge to dart his eyes frantically around but instead forced a smile and stared straight ahead at the congregation. His heart was thumping wildly and his palms were sweating profusely. John was almost sure that Jessie, whose hand he was holding would notice. His heart almost skipped a beat when out of the corner of his eye he spotted Malkia making a sudden movement. He relaxed when he saw her take out a hankie from her clutch bag and pat her face with it. She seemed to realise the effect that anxious moment had on him and cast him a smug look.

The wedding continued smoothly nonetheless.

John had hand written a love letter for his bride. He paused in between lines to look into her eyes as he spoke.

"Darling, you compliment me in every way. Every time you smile at me, it feels like the first time we met. Every moment with you is a delight. My most memorable one is when we first met. Your sense of adventure and passion about life inspires me and brings out that side of me. Our personalities are different in such a healthy way.

I'm addicted to you my dear. I will always be faithful to you. Thank you for always being there for me through the hard times and agreeing to share the rest of your life with me.

In you, I've not only found a best friend, but the treasure of a lifetime. I promise to love you forever."

By the time John had finished reading, the congregation's eyes were misty, including the reverend's. When Reverend George asked John if he would take Jessie as his lawfully wedded wife, he quickly said,

"I do." When it was Jessie's turn, she was overwhelmed by emotion. She thought about the vows they had just pronounced: "To have and to hold, for better or for worse, till death do us part."

These sounded like very serious statements to her. She was making a lifelong commitment. Butterflies floated in her bloated stomach; haunting voices lurked in her mind. *Are you sure till death?* Jessie managed to fight off the doubts and finally said yes after a pause. The crowd cheered wildly.

The couple exchanged rings and signed the marriage certificate solemnly. There was a final round of singing by the beautiful voices of the Anglican choir. As they sang, John bowed his head for a long time, dabbing at his eyes with his handkerchief. It all seemed surreal; the journey of his heart being broken over and over was finally over.

He had met the one. Or so he thought.

At exactly 1:00 pm, the MC took charge and gave instructions about the next part of the itinerary. He announced that lunch was served. The congregation streamed out, led by the bridal party. The guests sat at round tables at the green grounds. The bridal party took their place at the high table. The meal comprised of a sumptuous blend of bi-cultural cuisine: brown millet ugali, lots of traditional greens, plenty of goat meat as well as pilau, a popular coastal dish served in weddings, which is spicy rice cooked with pieces of meat inside depending on the generosity of the host.

The guests were treated to a round of traditional dances. The MC was good at his job and managed to convince even pot-bellied elderly men to hit the floor.

"Chini kwa chini, chini kwa chini," his voice boomed, bidding his dancers to go lower and lower, almost squatting as they danced.

By 3:00 pm, everyone was exhausted and it was time for gifts and speeches. Jessie's cousin gave a moving speech about how Jessie had hustled her way up in life and not depended on her parent's wealth or connections. Her father beamed with pride. Similar sentiments about John were echoed by one of his uncles, who had come all the way to Nairobi from Murang'a. He recounted with glowing admiration, John's struggles in raising enough capital to start his own business. John could feel his eyes get teary. His bride, sensing his emotion, squeezed his hand. He smiled appreciatively at her, as he thought of how lucky he was to be marrying an intelligent, kind and considerate woman.

A loud scream was heard from the centre of the tent. All eyes moved there. The boy who had sneaked into the wedding line-up was running as fast as he could towards the cake. By this time, his mother had caught sight of her son and started to chase him. Her husband joined in but they were too late. The little bundle of mischief had already plunged his face into one of the cakes that was part of the first tier of the wedding cake. Jessie was horrified, she stifled a scream.

"How exactly did the little horror manage to crash my wedding line-up?" She wondered.

She would have to talk to her cousin about him later. By this time, his parents had grabbed their son, whose cheeky grin now disappeared immediately he realised what was coming. As they carried him away from the wedding grounds, the stern looks on their faces told him that they did not share in his humour and his backside needed to get ready for a spanking"

Fortunately, the rest of the wedding cake was still intact and the wedding continued. As the cake was distributed to the guests, the women surrounded the couple and burst into a dance, swaying their hips jauntily to the rhythm. Jessie, who loved dancing but didn't know how, soon joined their movements, though hers were much slower, each step calculated. John on the other hand glided effortlessly across the grounds as though he was born a dancer; he took the lead, as he held her ever so gently and they moved together seamlessly.

The vote of thanks and closing prayers were carried on smoothly and at last the bridal party left the venue for their photo session at quarter past five.

Jessie and John were glad that it was over.

They went for their honeymoon in Greece. John surprised his new bride with a reservation in a beautiful hotel in Crete. Jessie thought they should live there forever; unfortunately, busy Nairobi was waiting for them, with its honking matatus and *wananchi* always in a hurry – as if the places would move if they did not scurry.

Jessie wondered what it would be like being John's wife. Did he remove his socks, dump one in one corner of the bedroom, and toss the other in the opposite direction? Thankfully, she had discovered during their honeymoon that he was not the snoring type. He had also not shown any signs of being disorganised...yet.

"How's the massage, hon?" John interrupted the quiet moment with the masseuse.

"Wonderful, dear. I wish it would never end!"

"Well, it had better, remember we came here together?" he smiled and winked.

"Okay, okay," Jessie reluctantly signalled to the masseuse that she was done with their session.

Silently turning the doorknob, she slipped out of the massage room as John helped Jessie get rid of the towel, wrapping her in her kikoy. They headed back to their room where Jessie slipped into a comfortable cotton sleeveless top, cut off shorts and canvas shoes.

John whistled as he eyed her behind mischievously. She pinched his arm and pretended to scold him but she was smiling, amused at her husband's catcall.

It was time for their evening walk. They stepped out into the fresh evening breeze, his arm protectively around her shoulder.

"If loving you is wrong, then I don't want to be right," John purred into her ear.

 "That is so cliché," Jessie laughed, remembering dozens of songs with that specific line, and a lanky, pimple-faced teenager also delivering that same pickup line to her, back in high school much to her disdain.

"But I mean it," John insisted.

They talked about anything and everything as they strolled. How many babies each wanted, the kind of house they would live in and whether they ought to have a dog or not. They both almost had the same things in common. The formerly pleasant breeze now became a biting wind. The lovebirds decided to call it an evening and head back to the hotel.

They stayed for a week in Greece and regretfully headed back to Kenya after a perfect honeymoon.

C H A P T E R   9

The transition into the couple's new home was smooth. Jessie relocated to Mombasa to join her husband in their new matrimonial home in an up-market Nyali estate. Jessie was the perfect, doting wife. She ensured that hot Swahili dishes awaited John when he returned from work. His days of living on avocados, sukuma wiki and bread were over. She kept the house spotless; his clothes had never been this clean in his life. John was a considerate, caring husband, rarely coming home empty-handed after work to his wife. He also never arrived home later than 7:00 pm.

Finding a suitable location for her kitenge business was an uphill task for Jessie. It took an entire month. during which she stayed home most of the days when she was not searching for a place. It was not easy on those days. The tension between the newly wedded couple began to grow.

It was a Thursday evening when John trudged into the house. He shook off his shoes, removed his shirt, socks and tie, tossing them on the floor. When Jessie emerged from the kitchen, she immediately frowned at the small pile in front of her husband, who did not appear to be moved. He was clutching at the tv remote, his eyes glued to the screen; he seemed oblivious to the mess around him. Jessie walked to the sofa where he was slumped and stood in front of him.

"You need to clear up after yourself," she sulked.

"I thought I now have a wife to do that for me," he said with a halfsmile but Jessie's expression made it disappear quickly.

"So do you think you married a slave?" she thundered.

"No-o-o," he stammered. "That's not what I meant…but it wouldn't hurt if my wife gave me a bit of TLC after a hard day's work." "Tender-loving-care my foot!" she shot back. "I could certainly do with some of that! Here I am, waiting on you day and night, and this is the thanks I get?"

"Honey, I'm really sorry," he stood up and held her by the shoulders.

"It's not easy being the sole provider for both of us," John confessed.

They both sat down on the sofa as John explained how the financial strain weighed heavily on him. As a man, he felt a dent in his self-esteem, which he, unfortunately, projected on his wife.

On the last day of the second month, they heard a knock on the door. It was the landlord, standing defiantly, his brow creased.

The embarrassment was too much to bear for John.

He pleaded with the landlord.

"Please give us a week. I promise I will pay the full amount in cash." The landlord stormed out but not without a final threat to throw them out if this promise was not kept. Cracks can be dangerous. Structural cracks endanger the stability of a building and may make it challenging to be rectified. A crack in a marriage can similarly cause things to fall apart, and the rift formed sometimes is irreconcilable.

On this particular day, the house was in shambles. Dishes lay stacked in the sink, covered with house flies. A thin film of dust enveloped almost every surface in their usually spotless apartment. This was the chaos that the new bride stepped into this particular evening after a long day at work. It would be an evening that would change things between Jessie and John forever.

Jessie felt all the energy drain out of her body like Coca Cola from the bottle into a thirsty mouth. She slumped onto the couch. Where was her husband? Was this what marriage was all about? Did he understand her need for companionship? Were they even compatible? Were their differences reconcilable? Jessie's head felt heavy; her eyes could not stay open. Then, at midnight, a loud, wild thumping at the front door caused Jessie's eyes to fly open.

It was John.

He had a lingering smell of beer on his breath and a funny look in his eyes. It was the first time he had gone out without her since they got married. Jessie also sensed a feminine scent on her husband's neck, not from any of her perfumes.

Her body froze.

"I-I I cccan explain," John said, slurring his words.

Jessie could not bring herself to talk. Instead, she nodded for him to go ahead. They sat down on opposite couches facing each other. It looked like they were both going to collapse, though for different reasons- one from being beleaguered and the other from being boozed.

 John began.

"I was going to hang out with the boys for a bit this evening. After all, I have never met them since the wedding."

Jessie took this information in carefully. It seemed reasonable to her since John had been busy at work, making up for the lost time during the wedding preparations, the wedding itself and the honeymoon. He also had to work harder to make ends meet as marriage comes with additional expenses, and Jessie was not working yet.

"But why did you have to stay out so late?" Jessie looked at her husband quizzically.

"Time flies when you're having fun. No one seemed to notice the time."

Jessie rolled her eyes.

"John, you're married now. You can't go around behaving like a teenager and hanging out with friends who are single."

Jessie's voice had a quiet exasperation to it.

"They're not all single. Mwangangi is separated," John said sullenly.

"That means he's technically single," his wife replied calmly.

John remained silent, fumbling with his phone. Jessie could not believe he had the nerve to be preoccupied with it in the middle of a fight. He was rubbing his nose as he did when nervous.

Its shrill ring startled them both. Jessie wondered who could be calling her husband. John's voice was low, reduced almost to a whisper as he responded in mono-syllables to the person on the other end of the line. Jessie wanted to laugh out loud at the absurdity of this; her husband's voice was usually loud and cheery when talking to his boys or clients.

"Umm... mmh," he grunted like a newborn piglet into the phone. Jessie rolled her eyes in disbelief.

"Sawa...all right," John concluded the conversation.

"Look hun. I don't like it when we fight. I'm really sorry. It won't happen again. That was one of the boys on the phone by the way."

John stood up and crossed over to his wife as he said this. He held both her hands and gently raised her to her feet. "Please forgive me sweetheart," he implored.

Jessie reluctantly accepted his apology, yet something lingered in her heart. Things were not going to end well. They both went to bed. There was nothing more to say.

For the next few weeks, their relationship was strained. It was a vicious cycle. Jessie did not feel loved. John did not feel respected. He often came home to a very moody wife. Jessie was constantly paranoid after that incident. She began checking her husband's phone for clues of philandering. John cleaned up his tracks too well. All his messages were suspiciously from men. Only one from a certain 'Mark' looked odd, but Jessie decided to let that one slide.

Jessie once heard a popular preacher say that it was a thousand times better to remain single than to marry the wrong person. She desperately hoped that she had not made a mistake in marrying John.

In the months that ensued, the couple seemed to drift apart slowly. One contributing factor was that Jessie finally found a location to set up her business. She no longer had time for her husband but focused all her energy on her company. She found that she was doing even better in Mombasa than in Nairobi. Here, the functions were more. The numerous weddings and celebrations made the demand for her clothes soar. Likewise, John concentrated all his efforts on his business. He spent all his weekends working, which Jessie had doubts about. Whenever Jessie questioned this, he responded by accusing her of not being understanding.

"Honey, don't you see that I'm trying to make more money for us, to give us a better life?" He often told her. Jessie learned to back off and retreat into silence.

Their marriage was definitely on the rocks.

C H A P T E R 10

The plane ride was short and smooth. Mombasa was only a fortyfive-minute flight from Nairobi. Jessie had relocated to live with her parents for some time to work out the issues in her marriage. She had left six months after the fight with John.

A trusted friend in Mombasa had offered to oversee her business in her absence. While in Nairobi, Jessie planned a trip with her friends, Samantha and Wabi, to go and visit her sister, Malkia, who also lived in Mombasa. Jessie figured that at least she could try and patch things up with another member of the family as she took a break from John.

The last time Jessie had seen her sister was at the wedding. Malkia had not been included in Jessie's line-up. The decision had not been an easy one. They had quarrelled weeks before the wedding. Malkia had thrown a tantrum about how the entire wedding had been set up. She refused to buy the dress design that Jessie had selected for the bridesmaids and walked out in a huff. She told Jessie she could replace her with one of her friends. Jessie had to leave Malkia out of the line-up, as she could foresee more drama, which was the last thing she needed.

Now, thinking how petty they had both been, she was filled with remorse. It was time to make amends. She hoped the resentment built up like ice in Malkia's heart had thawed.

This fall-out was not an isolated event.

Their relationship had suffered endless sibling rivalry. Malkia resented that Jessie, despite being the younger of the two, always managed to outdo her elder sister. It did not help either that when they were teenagers, Jessie ended up dating a boy Malkia had had a huge crush on. The boy had not reciprocated Malkia's feelings. This left a scar she had carried with her to adult life. Jessie had also been her daddy's favourite girl. Whenever she improved her grades in the slightest way, she was rewarded generously. For her eighteenth birthday, she had been given a beautiful, brand new, bright red BMW. Malkia went green with envy. And so, the resentment grew over the years, with Malkia constantly scheming up ways to get even. At last, her chance had finally come.

 As they disembarked from the plane, a sharp pain assaulted Jessie's heart. A lump rose in her throat.

"Wabi! Samantha! Let's take the next flight out of here, "Jessie said with a sense of urgency in her voice. Wabi gave her a look that suggested she was crazy.

"No way Jessie! We just got here," she replied indignantly.

Jessie tugged her arm restlessly, but Wabi ignored her. Samantha remained silent.

"We're not getting off this island until we have seen Malkia!" Wabi announced. Her voice rang with finality.

Jessie let out a sigh and grudgingly resumed trudging alongside her friends at the waiting bay. They gladly hopped in when their taxi arrived as the driver took their suitcases. Malkia lived quite a distance from the airport in Diani on the South Coast.

Diani Beach was a 17km stretch of soft, white sand, voted Africa's leading beach destination for the fifth time running since 2015.As Jessie gazed out of the window, admiring its beauty, she let the sound of the waves crushing against the coral reef and the gulls' rhythmic squawking lull her to sleep. Reality of scenes that had taken place before she slept crushed into her dreams. She dreamed of palm trees that stood on either side of the road, tall and proud like they had been there for eternity, of the small children who had waved at them as they drove past and of her friends, Wabi and Samantha, smiling and waving back.

They finally arrived at their destination, a beautiful house with serene surroundings. Jessie was jolted out of her sleep. The trio gaped at the impressive appearance of what lay before them - a massive, wrought iron gate with large brass handles. Malkia had done well for her age. She was only twenty-nine when she acquired the property. Always a hardworking young woman, she had started a wedding planning business, which was doing very well by all appearances.

The guard at the gate asked them to identify themselves. Then he saw Jessie's face, which seemed to trigger his memory. He smiled broadly but seemed unsettled, almost as though he did not want the ladies to enter.

"*Binti* Omwando! *Siku nyingi kweli, karibu sana!*" He said in refined Swahili.

"*Ahsante,*" replied Jessie.

The gates swung open, and they drove into what seemed to be an endless driveway, finally parking at the entrance of a huge, white three-storey house. Jessie thought it looked like one of the looming mansions in their neighbourhood that she enjoyed looking at when her father took her for drives from their music sessions; he played the piano while she sang.

A thought clouded her countenance, and her face fell as she remembered something disturbing. When they had been much younger, Malkia had stormed in during one of the piano sessions and burst into an angry tirade. She screamed that she felt side-lined in the family, and that no one had time for her.

"You know that's not true," her father had tried to tell her, but she would hear none of it. Jessie had no idea how to respond to these outbursts, which became more frequent with time.

The shrill sound of the doorbell ringing startled Jessie. She snapped out of her thoughts. Moments later, a tall silhouette loomed behind the door as it flew open. Jessie's flailing arms which had been spread wide with anticipation, ready to delve into the warm embrace of her older sister, hang limply at her sides. Jessie could not believe her eyes and for a moment, she thought she was slowly turning from a selfassured, intelligent being into a stark, raving madwoman. John, her John, stood before them, a towel wrapped around his waist, his chest bare. The prickly black hairs Jessie had often teased him about in their swimming escapades now seemed revolting.

A sing-song voice called out, "daaarling, you better come back in, or you'll catch a cold."

Jessie went numb at the sound of her sister's voice. She started to sway and John reached out to steady her.

"Get your filthy hands off me!" Jessie screamed.

John retreated quickly and stood like a statue, unsure of what to say. Malkia finally appeared in the hallway.

"I – I – wa-wasn't expecting you," was all Malkia could manage to stammer.

"Clearly," Jessie retorted, Hot angry tears streamed down her cheeks. She felt as if the whole world was spinning, everything spiralling out of control. Finally, unable to support her body any longer, her legs gave way, and she fainted. When she came to, her husband's face was peering anxiously into her own. Her frilly, chiffon blouse was wet where he and Malkia had poured water on her to resuscitate her.

There was only one way out of this situation. She slowly stood and barked an order, "Let's go!"

Wabi floated behind Jessie in a dream-like state, hardly believing what they had witnessed. She could not comprehend how people could be this cruel. All her life, she had grown up believing the best in everybody. This time, however, it was different.

On the other hand, Samantha, was in denial about the entire situation as she trudged behind Jessie and Wabi.

Wabi called a taxi to pick them up.

The trio rode in silence to the airport. Life without John seemed unimaginable to Jessie. Yet, the thought of his callous betrayal was too much to bear. Weirdly, the flight they had arrived on was the same one that flew them back to Nairobi.

The flight attendant looked genuinely surprised when they showed up on the same day with their heavy suitcases but mercifully said nothing. They took their seats, and a few minutes later, the plane was airborne. Jessie always slept through flights, no matter how short. This time, however, she could not sleep a wink. Samantha and Wabi fell asleep almost as soon as the plane took off, while Jessie remained wide-eyed, trying to piece how it had all happened. Slowly, everything started to come together like pieces of a puzzle. The busy weekends 'at work', the new wardrobe, the mysterious phone calls... it all started to make sense.

She felt another surge of anger rising, and tears welled up. She couldn't believe John had tried to put his slimy hands on her; this time around, no amount of soothing would restore the broken pieces. The conniving was finally over. Jessie eventually drifted off to a troubled sleep as she mused over the rude welcome that she had endured from her sister.

Once Jessie was back in Nairobi, the reality of her newly wedded husband's betrayal continued to sink in. She could not figure out what hurt her the most – the fact that he cheated on her with her sister or that he had committed adultery in the first place. Jessie had never pictured John as the promiscuous type all the time they had been dating. But then again, she had been blinded by love.

In the ensuing days, John made numerous attempts to contact Jessie, but his calls went unanswered. Eventually, Jessie blocked his number. The pain of hearing his voice was too much, and she knew she would never be able to forgive him for such a heinous act. She contemplated telling her parents, but she had no idea where to start. So she remained tight-lipped, mostly confined to her room, only coming out occasionally for meals with her parents. Jessie's tears flowed endlessly.

During these dark days, an even darker plot hatched in her mind.

John had to die for his sins.

C H A P T E R 11

Eventually, Jessie told her parents and John's family what had transpired between them. Jessie's parents were appalled at what had happened, while John's relatives were greatly astonished by his actions.

The fact that Malkia's name meant queen in Swahili was quite ironic. If anything, her behaviour was far from royal. Jessie had yet to come to terms with this level of betrayal from both her sister and the love of her life. The hurt in her heart was too much. She had her doubts about her husband but never in, her wildest dreams, expected or imagined that things would turn out like this.

Jessie had almost completely stopped eating. She lost ten kilos in one month. Jessie's father was furious about how her husband had treated. On the other hand, Jessie's mother, always a positive person by nature, was determined for a reconciliation to take place. She always believed the best in everyone and was convinced that where there was a will to sort things out, there was a way.

Mrs Omwando began to encourage her daughter to pick up her husband's calls. Jessie had not talked to John for a month since he shattered her world that fateful day.

At her mother's urging, she decided to hear him out eventually.

John called her at night, as he had previously been doing for a month, never tiring when she ignored his calls. He could not believe his luck this time when she picked up his call. His persistence finally wore out her resistance.

"Hello John," she sounded tired like all the fight was gone out of her. "Hello, Jessie. How are you doing?" John asked in a measured voice "Well thank you, and yourself?" Jessie tried to keep the sarcasm out of her voice, but it was hard to hide.

"I'm fine. I miss you Sweetie. I keep thinking about you all the time. Please give me a chance to explain. I can be in Nairobi by tomorrow."

Although John sounded very convincing, Jessie rolled her eyes. Who did John think he was to come prancing in and out of her life like that? And did he think that her heart was like a ball to be bounced around?

"Pppplease Jessie," John begged. "There are some things that you need to hear in person and I promise to stop bothering you after," he added in a meek voice.

This last part definitely appealed to Jessie. She was tired of his badgering, tired of having to ignore his calls. "Okay. But you will only have one hour."

"Great, thanks sweetie." John responded.

John packed an overnight bag immediately after the phone call, all the while thinking about how much of an idiot he had been to allow himself to be seduced by Malkia. It would take a lot of convincing to patch things up with his wife, but it was worth trying to salvage his marriage. The month without Jessie had been lonely. Things at his boat business had also not been that smooth. He remembered a Bible verse to the effect that God would answer his prayers if one treated his wife well. John was painfully aware that he was not in this group of privileged men. He was broke and unhappy. He booked a train for the next day. He left Mombasa by seven in the morning and was in Nairobi by noon.

John arrived at Jessie's parent's home soon after. He found one of his uncles who had been part of the dowry negotiations waiting for him, having arrived some minutes before him.

Mr Omwando greeted them coldly, but his wife was cordial. "Gentlemen, do come in. *Karibuni.* Welcome," she urged.

The visitors felt more at ease with this kind lady than with her husband. The dining table was already set and they all took their places around it. Mrs Omwando had prepared some samosas and tea. Jessie joined them. She shook hands with the visitors and sat down opposite her husband. The conversation was light. Once they had their brunch, Mr.
Omwando broached the subject that had convened them.

"As you all know, the reason we have gathered here today is not a good one. I will allow John to lead the discussion and we will take it from there."

"I am terribly sorry about everything that has happened and deeply regret the sorrow it has caused to my wife here as well as the embarrassment to the entire family. All I want is a chance to work things out with my wife. Life has been extremely difficult since we separated. I have since completely disconnected myself from Malkia and humbly beg for Jessie's forgiveness." He paused briefly to clear his throat, his eyes watering. Then, he looked directly at his wife.

"Sweetie, please forgive me. I have done a lot of soul searching. I cannot envision spending the rest of my life without my wife. I have been so lonely this past month without you."

Jessie looked contemptuously at him.

"I'm not sure what to believe anymore. I was foolish enough to believe the vows you made during our wedding and the promise to love me forever," Jessie retorted.

"I never stopped loving you my dear." John responded.

At this juncture, John's uncle spoke up.

"I agree that what happened is indeed unfortunate and grievous. However, according to culture, John has two choices in such circumstances. To marry the woman he has become involved with, hence, a polygamous marriage, or make amends with his wife and discard the other woman completely. John has chosen the latter and will have to pay a hefty fine to you, Jessie's parents. He and Jessie will have to discuss with the reverend who oversaw the wedding - how they both feel about a future together after this experience. The reverend will walk them through the journey of forgiveness and reconciliation. They would additionally have several meetings with the pastors who gave them pre-marital counselling. This will have to happen as soon as possible. Do you, John and Jessie agree to this?

John nodded slowly. Jessie was still unsure but finally agreed

Mrs. Malesi offered to pray before the group was dismissed.

* * * * *

Jessie attended several counselling sessions with her husband before she realised that their marriage would not work. Jessie no longer felt like they were compatible. She also could not bring herself to ever trust her husband again and was not willing to continue living under the same roof.

He had proved to be a husband of the wind.

Jessie went back to Mombasa, packed her things, closed her business and relocated to Nairobi, back to her apartment in Westlands after her tenant, an immigrant, announced that she would be returning home to her country. This meant that Jessie did not have to stay with her parents. Talk of perfect timing.

# CHAPTER 12

It took Jessie several weeks to actually believe that what she had seen in Mombasa was real. Her husband had betrayed her. Not with some strange woman, but her own sister. She began to envision John in a coffin.

Jessie had never thought about committing murder in her whole life even though being an avid reader, she had read thrillers whose twisted plots were entirely based on murder. She began meditating on a suitable plot to eliminate John. Jessie decided that an accident would have to be staged. It would be easiest if it involved an aspect of John's usual routine; a boating accident at his place of work, a surprise attack at his home – perhaps strangulation while he slept; or have someone spike his drink with a lethal portion that would put him to sleep forever. She concluded that a less messy death would be better.

After weeks of researching, Jessie decided on a car accident.

She made a deal with a professional assassin called Tom. Jessie gave him a duplicate set of the keys to John's garage. The plan was for Tom to sneak in one day and puncture the car tyres. The slow puncture would initially be unnoticed but fatal to the driver, when at last the air came out and the deflated tyres did their lethal work.

* * * * *

Jessie carefully placed her drink – a cold glass of orange juice on the glass coffee table and reached for her cell phone. She dialled a number and waited.

On the third ring, a gruff voice answered, "Hallo?"

"C'est moi"

The voice seemed genuinely delighted "Ahhh, Jess! *Comment ça va?*

"I am doing well thank you, and you?"

"Oui, moi aussi!"

Jessie had taken a basic French course some time back and it was in moments like this that she was grateful she had. "Tell me, what can I do for you, my dear?"

"It's a long story Tom. Do you have time to meet?"

"Bien sur! Anything for you my dear."

"Ok, tomorrow evening at six, Westlands? I know a nice coffee shop at the mall."

"Pas de problème.., I look forward to seeing you."

Tom was an old friend, who learnt French from years of living in Congo and frequent trips to France. Jessie doubted the voyages to France, but could not really disprove them. Tom had dubious ways for surviving. If you needed anything, he had it. He was a jack of all trades. From black market currencies to imported cars, he practically dealt with everything. It was even rumoured among Tom's friends that if you had someone who had rubbed you the wrong way, he could organise a couple of hit men to 'take care of things for you'. Jessie had heard about this last part but had never confirmed it. This was the reason for their meeting the following evening. She wanted to know if Tom could help her with John's issue. She felt some relief as she pressed the 'end call' button. Perhaps, this could be the solution to her thirst for revenge. She poured more juice and smiled. *You have no idea what you have coming, sweetheart,* she thought to herself.

Jessie was at the Maridadi café where they had agreed to meet the next day promptly at 6:00 pm. She wore a simple, black chiffon dress with a grey, silk scarf and no make-up, to match the sombre mood of the occasion. Tom was already there, sitting at a dark corner. His hooked teeth jutted out like a warthog.

He was puffing away a thick cigar. The supposed gun for hire rose as soon as he saw her and pecked her on both cheeks.

"Good to see you!" he exclaimed.

"Likewise," Jessie replied

He stood back a moment, assessing Jessie. "You've lost weight and you don't look well. Is something the matter?"

"Well, it's a long story, and I'm not sure I can stand through the whole of it..." Jessie responded with a wry smile.

"Of course, please, sit."

They both sat and ordered double café lattès, with creamy white froth. Tom ordered a beef sandwich too. Maridadi café had a warm glow around that made one immediately feel at home as soon as one walked in. It had a laid back ambience, decorated with African art pieces, basketry and potted plants all around.

A waiter lit candles all around and the ambiance was enhanced even more.

"It's John, my husband. Remember him?"

"How could I forget him? I came to your wedding"

"Of course. Anyway, I no longer feel the same way about him, to put it mildly. Actually, I would very much like to fulfil my vows and part. I want him dead."

Tom heard sentiments like this from clients all the time. Still, he was somehow taken aback to see what Jessie had become. He had always known her to be a warm, caring person, her earnest face oozing naivety in a sweet, childlike manner. Now her face was set like a flint-cold and determined. A real ice-queen.

"Tell me how you want me to take care of him."

Jessie narrated how she spent sleepless nights, researching on the plan, reading about murders and how to cover up her tracks. Tom sunk his warthog teeth into a giant-sized sandwich, chomping noisily as he listened.

"It's a fool proof plan. I think you should consider changing your career," Tom said smiling, approvingly when she finished explaining her plan.

"It's a deal. I'll leave for Mombasa tomorrow." Jessie stood and offered him her hand. He shook it warmly, paid for their coffees and waited a few minutes for her to go before he left. He did not want to arouse any suspicion, and certainly did not want anyone linking him to the murder.

* * * * *

The accident was gruesome.

John had struggled to control his speeding car when the tyres burst.

Glass sprayed everywhere as the windscreen shattered. The airbags, which usually would have helped, could not save him this time. As he lay in anguish inside the wrecked Toyota Premio, John saw his whole life fleeting before him. He remembered questioning God the reason for his suffering. The answer came now.

Jessie...

He felt deeply in his soul, that somehow after his death, Jessie would be a blessing to many. He also felt she had done something bad to him, but he could not for the life of him figure out what it was. It did not matter now.

"Forgive her Lord," he murmured, stopping to draw a deep breath, his eyes tightly closed, his hands clenched in fists. It felt like he was being pulled apart in several directions. Blood flowed freely from his body. John sensed he did not have much time.

"I'm sorry Lord for all the bad things I have done in my life. Please forgive me and save me. I commit my soul to you Jesus," John prayed.

As John uttered these words, he felt a rush of wind engulf him, comfortingly. He felt at peace in a way he had never experienced in his life.

"Auuu-uuu! Njooni haraka! Kuna mtu amefariki ndani ya gari!" a passerby screamed.

In five minutes, a crowd surrounded the wrecked car in a frenzied hurry. A shrill scream pierced the air as someone recognized John's marred face.

"Ni John, yule mwanabiashara!."

There was more wailing and screaming as a fire broke out in the car's engine.

"*Ondokeni*!" someone yelled.

The crowd scurried away as the car exploded, flames engulfing the whole car.

Tom stood watching at a distance, a smirk on his face. He was satisfied that the job had been completed. He got into his car and called Jessie. "The job is done"

"Good job."

* * * * *

The police found John charred remains after the fire was put off. John's face was mangled with parts of the silver Premio. The crowd turned away their faces from the gruesome scene as the police removed the body from the burnt car. They huddled around the accident scene, whispering to each other, speculating what could have led to this unfortunate turn of events.

The police found John's phone undamaged in the accident scene. They scrolled through his cell phone and spotted a number saved under 'wifey' and called it.

"Hello," a woman answered on the first ring.

"My name is Inspector Madondo."

"Yes, Inspector Madondo. Why are you calling me using my husband's phone? Wait! Where is my husband? Is he there with you?"

"Where are you?" Inspector Madondo inquired, fielding off Jessie's questions.

"In Nairobi. What's going on!"

"Is it possible for you to come to Mombasa? We would like you to speak with you in person."

"Why? Where is my husband!"

"Madam, please, make arrangements and come to Mombasa. This is an urgent issue and it is better if we speak in person. I am sending you a Google map pin. When you arrive, call me through this number."

"But-"

"I know you have a lot of questions, Madam. I will answer them when you arrive. In the meantime, try to take it easy," Inspector Madondo interrupted the woman on the other end of the phone.

"O-okay," she conceded.

"Thank you for your patience, Madam. I have just sent the Google map pin. I will be waiting," Inspector Madondo said and hung up. She had sent to Jessie a Google map pin of a restaurant close to the morgue they planned to take the deceased body.

* * * * *

Jessie arrived later that evening. She had managed to get the last flight from Nairobi.

The airport taxi dropped Jessie on the pinned location. Inspector Madondo was there as promised.

The inspector led Jessie to a corner table.

""Mrs. Karanja, I'm afraid I don't have very good news for you," Mr Madondo began as he tried to see through the dark sunglasses that Jessie was wearing.

Jessie's heart pounded with every word the inspector uttered, despite knowing what he was about to disclose to her.

"Inspector, enough with the preambles already. You made me travel all the way from Nairobi to Mombasa. Out with it already!"

"Mrs Karan-"

"Please. Just tell me," Jessie implored.

Inspector cleared his throat. "Mrs. Karanja, I'm afraid I don't have very good news for you. "Your husband was involved in a terrible accident."

"No! That can't be!" Jessie screamed, removing her sunglasses. "No! No! My husband was okay the last time I talked to him yesterday. How could this be?" Jessie asked, screaming In anguish, not caring that all the other patrons in the restaurant were staring at her.

"Mrs Karanja please calm down," Inspector Madondo tried calming the hysterical woman who just some minutes ago looked composed as she stepped out of the taxi, wearing an expensive, fitting, linen skirt suit. He did not know much about fashion but the way she carried herself reeked of class and elegance.   As she continued screaming, he was not sure anymore.

Unearthly screams emanated from her throat. Even though she was acting, the horror of John's death finally hit her.

Inspector Madondo let her cry it out and when she seemed a bit calm, he narrated in detail the accident that had ended her husband's life. After, he took Jessie to the morgue to view the body and begin the paperwork.

The accident had happened along Nyali Bridge, close to Jessie's matrimonial home. This meant several people who knew the couple were in the vicinity when the accident happened. Some had heard of the devastating news as they arrived home from work. They were supportive of Jessie. They stayed with her up until late into the night, keeping her company, but finally one by one, they trickled back to their homes.

The police sealed off the accident scene for two more days before they were satisfied that they had done a comprehensive investigation and unsealed the area.

John's relatives on hearing of his demise immediately started making plans for his funeral. Some of his relatives arrived from Nairobi the next day along with Jessie's parents, Samantha and Wabi.

A week later, Jessie was staring blankly at the coffin. Her dark grey hat mercifully shielded her dry eyes. Her hands rested on her long, black chiffon dress as she crossed her legs, revealing a pair of black, suede pumps.

She tried to piece together how her life had come to this. Nothing seemed to make sense anymore. Her mouth felt unexpectedly dry. Theirs had seemed like a bright future ahead, with a wonderful marriage. Now, she was left with nothing but crushed dreams and shattered hopes. Surely, life could not have dealt her such cruelty, Jessie thought..It all seemed like one big, sick joke – the way he had taken her love for granted and callously stabbed her in the back.

Jessie made a show of dabbing at her eyes as she gripped her mother's hand tightly while sympathisers came up to her, one after another, to offer their condolences. She mastered a grateful smile through her 'tears' and wished the whole ceremony could end as quickly as it had begun as she contemplated her life without John. Elation washed over her.

93

JEAN WAIRIMU KAMINA

C H A P T E R   13

Jessie decided to extend her stay in Mombasa, though she could not get herself to stay in her matrimonial home after John's death. A friend had offered her a guest room in her beachfront villa.

The heinous act of murder still haunted Jessie, lurking at the back of her mind and resurfacing whenever she was by herself, especially when she took long walks on the beach each day. She could not believe that she had committed murder; it seemed inconceivable and even illogical for her to do a thing like that. Yet she had.

As much as her new life allowed her to move on, she could not help feeling weighed by hopelessness and the absurdity of the whole situation. She still had some flashbacks from her past life with her husband. That sent her emotions reeling, fresh waves of sadness hitting her hard. She constantly wondered how long it would take her to really move on.

On the flip side, she was relieved that things had moved smoothly according to plan. Tom had been meticulous in his work. Not a single trace of evidence was left; nothing that could trace the accident back to her.

She sighed with contentment as she sipped her *mnazi*. It tasted different from her usual choice of wine, but she did not mind the taste of the strong fermented local brew. Nor did she care much about the drink's social construct- of older men partaking in it as they debated pertinent issues, sitting around leisurely in a circle. She just wanted to exist in oblivion; all her cares tossed to the wind.

On one of her walks, Jessie found herself lying on a trail on the beach where she and John had taken numerous walks when they were dating. She was lost in her memories of her and John when the shrill ring of her phone interrupted her. She wondered who it could be as her mother and housekeeper were the only people who had the number.

* * * * *

Back in Nairobi, on the day that Jessie had met up with Tom, unknown to them both, someone had seen them at the restaurant. It was someone with whom John had done business with in the past. His name was Mutasia. He was very curious about precisely what Jessie could be discussing with a man of ill-repute. He knew Tom was a killer as he had seen many wanted signs that promised a hefty reward for whoever found him.

However, he also knew that Jessie and John were separated, and so whoever Jessie hung out with or dated was none of his business. Upon hearing the news of John's accident though, he knew that John would probably still be alive if he had made it his business. So he felt that he owed his dead business acquaintance one favour; to make sure his killer was behind bars forever.

Mutasia made a phone call to a detective he knew who worked in Nairobi, called Mwindi. He described Tom as a bald, middle-aged, six foot, slim brown-skinned man with a thick moustache and a limp.

The detective confirmed that he knew Tom very well. He told Mutasia that Tom was a wanted criminal and had been after he escaped from prison a long time ago. The fact that a man died after his wife interacted with Tom was worth investigating; the detective told Mutasia. He intended to start investigating Jessie and see what he could come up with

Detective Mwindi visited Jessie's house in Westlands the following day. He posed as a desperate cousin and told the housekeeper who answered the door that he urgently needed to see Jessie. The housekeeper informed him that Jessie had gone to Mombasa and that she would not be back for some time. The detective looked disappointed as he confided in her that he did not even have enough money to go back to the village. He was dressed in a shabby t-shirt, faded jeans and old dusty shoes. Nevertheless, he convinced her to give him Jessie's number. Detective Mwindi was very surprised when she complied, as people in this city generally did not trust strangers. He thanked the housekeeper profusely and left in a hurry. He found a quiet spot and made a call to Jessie. He pretended to be a longlost former student in the technical college where Jessie had studied fashion design. The detective made it sound like he was dying to see her and catch up, and was also in Mombasa. Jessie could not remember him. However, since she did not want to appear rude, she agreed to meet him briefly for coffee the next day.

Mwindi took the night bus to the Coast and arrived the following morning. He checked into a modest lodging and changed into a grey suit. He wore a brown leather belt and matching shoes. He was also very good looking, which added to his overall charm. He showed up promptly at the coffee shop where Jessie had suggested they meet. It was not hard to find her. She was the only woman sitting by herself, and like Mwindi, she was not lacking in the looks department. He shook her hand warmly as if he had known her all her life – which he had not. They had tea and *mahamri*, a popular snack at the coast. They chatted amicably until Mwindi gently broached the subject of John's murder. He was stunned when Jessie's eyes became piercingly cold. Her breathing became laboured, and she clenched her hands into tight fists. At that moment, Mwindi felt real fear and was sure that he would turn into a punching bag for Jessie very shortly.

Then, just as suddenly as the transformation had taken over Jessie, it stopped. Jessie unclenched her fists, leaned back, and shrugged her shoulders nonchalantly.

"He's been dead for a month now," she casually told him. "It was a car accident. I always told him to check all the tires before driving off." "But Jessie, how did you know that the cause of the accident was faulty tires? Didn't the press say that it was a head-on collision?"

Mwindi was now looking intently at her. Jessie looked momentarily flustered but recovered quickly.

"Yes, that's true," she said, "I guess I must have been reading too many murder novels," she responded with a nervous laugh.

Detective Mwindi stayed at the Coast for another month. During this time, he engaged his team, who investigated Jessie. They found out that she had made several calls to the hitman – which they recorded as evidence. Detective Mwindi also had the record of his first meeting with Jessie, which he intended to use as another piece of evidence. He additionally instructed one of his boys to call her to see if they could get more proof of murder from her. She picked on the first ring. "*Vipi* Jess?" A male voice said in a cheerful voice. "Enjoying your little holiday in Mombasa raha?"

"*Nani huyu?*" Jessie hissed as a familiar dizzying feeling crept through her.

"It doesn't matter. What matters right now is that you, darling, are in a lot of trouble. You know it's not a nice thing to eliminate one's husband ," he sounded disapproving.

Jessie's blood froze. The dizzy feeling intensified her legs gave way under her.

"Anyhow, my boys are on their way to pick you up. Sorry for cutting the holiday short. However, there's always a price to pay for every evil deed, isn't there?"

The phone clicked dead before Jessie could respond. Wild thoughts circulated in her head. She had done everything to cover her tracks. Who could have sold her out?

She began to run to the beach house she had rented out after she moved out from her friend's place. She did not stop until she was inside and had bolted the door. She packed some of her things hastily into a black bag- her passport, a wad of money and a change of clothes. She ran out again, tossed the bag into the car she had rented and hastily drove to Mombasa International Airport. She barely managed to get a seat in an aeroplane heading for Nairobi, but luckily, another passenger cancelled his flight last minute. She intended to fly to Nairobi and then proceed to Rwanda. Jessie knew no one there, but that was a small matter, considering what was at hand.

Jessie sat down at the waiting lounge and drew her black scarf further over her head, counting the minutes to when she could board the aeroplane. Then, eerily like John's, a deep, husky voice whispered, "you can run, but you can't hide."

Jessie passed out. She was immediately surrounded by police officers who whisked her away from the crowd that had started gathering around them. Mwindi and two detectives carried her to the waiting car outside and drove to Makupa police station in Mombasa.

CHAPTER 14

Jessie stared forlornly at the ceiling of the cheerless remand cell where they had locked her in.

She had never been arrested before. At the door, a female police officer frisked her and relieved her of her precious jewellery, passport, watch, money and cell phone. Next, Jessie had to sign in the occurrence book, or OB, as it is popularly called. It was a big, black book with pages that had started to turn yellow and fold at the edges. The other prisoners were mainly street girls, picked up mostly on prostitution charges and drug peddling. One girl smiled warmly at her. She could not have been more than eighteen.

"Hujambo," she greeted Jessie in fluent Swahili.

"Sijambo," Jessie responded, ever so conscious of her Nairobi accented Swahili. Watu wa bara, or people from the mainland, was how the people at the coast referred to outsiders. However, the girl was not condescending in her manner but had a curious demeanour

about her. *"Jina langu ni Halima, na nimeletwa hapa kwa sababu ya ukahaba."* Halima did not look the least bit embarrassed by this fact. On the contrary, her beautiful, dark eyes were unflinching.

She proceeded to share with Jessie the intricate details of her arrest, and how her client, a wealthy, prominent man, had refused to remunerate her after offering her 'services'. When Halima threatened to spread the word to the close-knit community around them, the man decided he had to do something about it. He could not risk the damage this would bring to his reputation. He did not seem to care that she was also his client; - he kept her hooked on drugs.

He had her arrested on prostitution charges.

Halima now looked expectantly at Jessie, as if after having poured out her heart in that manner, an exchange of stories was only fair. Jessie gulped and, on an afterthought, decided she had nothing to lose. She explained that her husband had been an evil man and deserved to die. Halima listened, and after Jessie finished narrating her story, she told Jessie she would have done the same thing if she had been in her place.

"Hawa wanaume wa siku hizi hawana adabu." she offered, her full lips pouting.

John did not deserve to be spared and was probably being *nyama choma* in hell.

Halima and Jessie's conversation was suddenly cut short when the sour-looking guard arrived.

"Simameni! Malaya nyinyi!" The guard barked at them.

Jessie was fuming with rage at this insult, but Halima was amused by this reference to her profession and tried hard to suppress laughter.

The guard jerked open the cell door and tersely told Jessie to go out to the visitors' area. Her lawyer had arrived and wanted to begin working on the trial right away.

He was a polite young man with a Kikuyu accent. His stylish grey Armani suit and expensive cologne reeked of money and class. Jess could see her face in his meticulously polished, black leather shoes. All this was in stark contrast to the smelly remand cell where the women were being held. Jessie was, however, unmoved. She was used to money and a lot of it- Halima, though was not. Her alluring mouth was wide-open as she stared at him.

"Hello, Jessie," he said, extending his hand in greeting. Jessie shook it cautiously as though it would break. His eyes crinkled, and the corners of his mouth turned upwards in a relaxed smile.

"I am Kamau. *Razima utatoka mahari hapa*," he promised in a thick Kikuyu accent.

Jessie could not agree more. She had to get out of prison ASAP!

They sat down. Kamau insisted he tell him everything. She did, but conveniently left out the part about the hitman hire.

"How exactly did John die, Jessie?" Kamau was frowning, trying to piece together the bits she had told him so far.

"The poor thing had an accident. He was in the wrong place at the wrong time," Jessie sounded unconvincing, even to herself.

Kamau sighed. She was a lousy liar, and he could already predict just how difficult this case could get in court.

However, he forced himself to smile at her.

"I need details, Jessie, which may determine how and where you are going to spend the rest of your life after this case.

Her eyes widened as though he was telling her about a nuclear weapon he had just discovered. She was not only a lousy liar but a lousy actor. She was not fooling anyone, and Kamau was getting impatient, drumming his thick fingers on the prison table. They sat on cold, uncomfortable metal chairs, and every minute seemed like an hour to him.

"Well, I first heard of the unfortunate incident from a detective… Detective Madondo."

Kamau jotted the name down in his notebook and made a mental note to talk to the detective immediately.

"Go on, please," he urged when Jessie stopped talking. She appeared to be choking back what were definitely crocodile tears.

"The detective said that John had been found in a pool of blood. The car had spun out of control. They said his tires had been punctured." She chose her words carefully.

"Punctured? Kamau's thick eyebrows were raised. You mean, it was a set-up, Jessie?" Kamau asked?

"He was such a sweet man." Jessie was lying through her teeth and hoped that this lawyer was not one of the human lie detectors she had met in the past.

The only problem was that Kamau did not believe a word of what she had said. He was going to need plausible evidence to build a case to defend his client, whose lips seemed incapable of uttering a single honest statement.

His patience was running thin.

"Well, John had enemies. He was a successful business man who had built up his boat business from scratch." "Boat?" Kamau inquired.

"Yes, he hired out speed boats in Mombasa." Jessie could see it all now, how John had all the time to see her sister while away on 'business'. She felt the anger slowly rising in her but tried to keep her calm. Kamau did not seem to notice. She continued her story.

"Business was going really well, and as you can imagine, not everyone is happy when one is doing well. I didn't really meet his business associates because he told me he preferred to keep his family and business separate. This made sense to me at the time. Shortly before his death, John had received some threats over the phone. He seemed extremely troubled by them." "Did he go to the police?'

"No, he thought they wouldn't have helped much."

"Did he tell you who was threatening him?" Kamau had to be pushy in his probing as it became clear that Jessie did not want to talk.

He finally left the cell with a promise to keep Jessie updated on any upcoming developments.

Jessie had a million things on her mind.

"He didn't believe a word I said. If my lawyer doesn't believe me, how will I be able to convince an entire jury and judge?"

C H A P T E R 15

Days turned into weeks as investigations progressed. Several witnesses took turns on the stand. They all seemed to have a common theme; the accident had been a tragedy; John was a careful driver, and his death had been quite unfortunate.

Finally, the court date arrived. Jessie looked pale and tired as she was led into the courtroom by the prison warden. She had cleaned up well, but unfortunately, not even her favourite grey and peach pin-striped suit could disguise the bag of bones that formed her frame. It was rare that a prisoner was allowed in without prison clothes before being acquitted. However, she was not sure she would get to the release point. Kamau's doubts clouded her already troubled mind. She might not have been so careful after all.

As she sat down, she felt the jury's eyes on her; Jessie slowly lifted her face so she could see them. Several married women looked sympathetically at her, perhaps wondering how life would be if their husbands died. Jessie then locked eyes with her parents, seated on the same bench as her friends Samantha and Wabi. It was comforting to see them.

Two key witnesses had yet to give their testimony. A hush fell over the entire courtroom as they arrived on the scene. At first, Jessie could not make out who they were until she completely turned her head to focus on them. Then, when she saw the first witness, she gasped. Kamau reached out his hand to steady her.

"Oh my God… Malkia!" were her last words before she passed out.

Anxious onlookers turned into emergency advisors – everyone wanting to give an opinion on how Jessie should be handled. The judge, however, decided she had had enough of the circus and pounded her gavel suddenly on her desk.

"Order!"

The courtroom was silent just as Jessie regained consciousness. Thoughts came flooding back to her; the scene felt like a second betrayal, which it was. John's 'former schoolmate' and Jessie's sister. Betrayal all over again!

Malkia looked unconcerned.

The cross-examination began.

"Do you have reason to believe that your sister could have murdered her husband?" The prosecution lawyer, Mr Tausi, inquired.

"Yes," Malkia said unflinching in her response.

"Could you tell us more?" He continued, oblivious to the tremor he had just caused.

"Sure." Malkia proceeded to talk about the issues that John had shared with her about his marriage. How miserable he had been with Jessie and how unsupportive she had been.

"My sister is a very controlling and jealous person," she told the court. "To the extent she would murder her husband?" Mr Tausi inquired.

"Yes. John was always walking on eggshells around Jessie. On one occasion, he told me how he came home from socialising with his friends and Jessie went berserk. "

"Miss Malkia, it seems you and the deceased were very intimate. Could you please tell the court the nature of your relationship?"

"We were lovers."

The courtroom gasped. The married women on the jury did not look amused.

"It's not my fault. John was weak. He should have controlled himself." "Objection, your honour!" Kamau was furious. "Let the witness stick to the relevant details."

"Sustained," said the judge.

Mr Tausi looked apologetic. "Miss Malkia, did John ever disclose that he feared for his life because of his wife?"

"Yes, He told me that if Jessie ever found out about us, he'd be a dead man."

"That's all, your honour." Mr. Tausi sat down.

Kamau stood and approached the witness stand.

"Miss Malkia, do you remember when and where John told you he was afraid for his life? And were those his exact words?"

"Yes, I remember it as if it was yesterday. We are in my house. John had left work but was reluctant to return home and face his lunatic wife. Those were his exact words."

After Malkia's testimony, the courtroom adjourned for recess.

Then the proceedings resumed; the verdict was a rude shock for Jessie, even though she had not expected anything less. She was found guilty of first-degree murder. John's family looked visibly pleased, and his friends gave her a gloating look. She burst into tears, but there was no sympathy from most of the onlookers.

Jessie's father shot up from his chair, shaking his fist.

"I believe my daughter is innocent!" he yelled.

"Order!" shouted the judge.

Mrs Omwando held his hand and gently led him out of the building. They were flanked on both sides by Jessie's friends.

C H A P T E R   16

After being found guilty of the murder of her husband, Jessie was sentenced to life imprisonment in Lang'ata Women's Maximum Prison.

Her world came crashing down. How could she and Tom have been so careless? She read in the *Daily Nation* that Tom had escaped the country and was a wanted criminal.

She never heard from him again.

As she shuffled along, being led away in handcuffs, the shackles on her feet were heavier than before. She was grateful that she had no children. How would she have been able to explain the situation to them –that mummy was a murderer?

The prison doors clang shut. Jessie was left alone in the dark prison of her soul as bitter tears slid down her face. The future looked very bleak. A smell of rotting flesh, specifically of rats, hang in the air. She tried to hold her nose to avoid the choking smell, but this did not seem like a sustainable idea. She needed to breathe.

That night, Jessie refused to eat anything. Not that there was a wide variety of dishes to choose from. This was undoubtedly no five-star hotel, nor was it anything like those amazing restaurants she was so fond of patronising.

The warden had brought in semi-cooked ugali and boiled beans. The revolting sight of fat weevils floating around the beans was too much for Jessie. She emptied all the contents of her earlier meal right onto the plate.

The prison warden who had brought her the food was not impressed.

"Itabidi uzoee madam," she snarled. Jessie knew she never would. She kept waking up at different night hours, at midnight, three in the morning, and finally six o'clock.

Breakfast was thin, watery porridge with no accompaniment, or *'kifuniko'* popularly known in Kenya. For the coming days, the routine was the same. Sometimes Jessie felt like it would have been better if she had been given a death sentence. It felt like the last days mentioned in the Bible. Where people asked for death, but none was forthcoming.

However, little did she know that all that was about to change in less than two months.

One Sunday, the prisoners were gathered together for a church service.
A visiting pastor from Ukumbani was preaching.

The prisoners were slowly streaming in; the atmosphere was charged. They sang several praise songs, and then the worship leader took over the next session. For no apparent reason, Jessie felt hot tears begin to stream down her cheeks.

"What is wrong with me?" she wondered aloud.

A fat woman was quizzically staring at her. And as Jessie stared right back at her, she saw the words: "FORGIVEN" clearly in her head. The song 'Amazing Love' was playing simultaneously too. "Amazing love, how could it be that you, my king, would die for me." She was thinking of all the sins she had committed in her lifetime such as the 'white' lies to her mum, shoplifting in supermarkets, coming home with unfamiliar stationery and now, the more recent grievous, crime of murdering her husband. How could God forgive someone like her?

The word surfaced again. This time, Jessie could hear it resounding inside her. The tears continued streaming down her cheeks.

The scriptures that the pastor was reading seemed tailor-made for her, especially for her.

"John 14:6 Jesus said to him, "I am the way, the truth, and the life. No one comes to the Father except through Me." John 3:16 "For God so loved the world that He gave His only begotten Son, that whoever believes in Him should not perish but have everlasting life." Romans 4:6- "Blessed are those whose lawless deeds are forgiven, and whose sins are covered; blessed is the man to whom the Lord shall not impute sin."

She could not bring herself to accept these words from the scripture. For her, people had to pay for their sins. Her ex-husband had died for his sins. However, these Christians seemed to believe in one man dying for the sins of others. She wondered why on earth anyone would want to do that. The more the worship leader sang, the heavier Jessie's heart grew. Soon, she found herself walking down the aisle to the front of the room. She felt a pair of soft arms lovingly embrace her as she wept uncontrollably.

More curious prisoners surrounded them, gawking openly.

The pastor asked Jessie the pertinent question: "Would you like to receive Jesus Christ as your Lord and saviour of your life? The female usher hugging her now loosened her hold on Jessie as if to somewhat give her breathing space to ponder the question. Jessie inhaled, then exhaled sharply. She was still struggling to understand how anyone could forgive someone like her, let alone be in a relationship with her. Jessie was overcome by emotion at the thought of such profound love, the lengths God would go to for a single soul, especially one as horrible as hers.

"Yes, I am," she said.

The pastor told Jessie to repeat after him the sinner's prayer, "I confess that I am a sinner." As Jessie said it, she could not help feeling this was an understatement. However, as she continued praying. However, as she continued to pray, Jessie felt a heavy weight lifted from her shoulders and float away from her. She felt lighter than she had ever felt in her life.

She was forgiven.

Some years back, she would have been driving home drunk as a skunk in the wee hours of the morning, gingerly balancing a Tusker beer bottle with one hand and the steering wheel with the other, as a throbbing headache ripped through her forehead. Now here she was, lightheaded, literally without a care in the world as she had cast them all to Jesus. Jessie could not believe how much time she had lost pursuing meaningless pleasures rather than eternal treasures.

She now recounted the events of that night. When her decision to be saved was announced, people clapped seemingly indefinitely. However, a small voice in her head kept nudging her, "Do you really think that God forgives murderers?" Another disturbing thought, "I don't feel saved".

Yet something in Jessie was very different in the days following that experience. She had a new gait in her walk, a sparkle in her eyes, and a glow on her face that even the other prisoners seemed to notice. Jessie no longer experienced mood swings and panic attacks that had tormented her before.

* * * * *

When Jessie shared the news of her salvation with her mother in a letter, Mrs Omwando was elated to hear about her daughter's divine transformation. Being a firm believer, Mrs Omwando had been praying for God to touch her daughter's heart for many years. Finally, God had answered her prayers. Even if it had taken the incarceration of Jessie for her to experience the turnaround, her mother felt that the scripture in Romans 8:28 rang true: "And we know that all things work together for good to those who love God, to those who are the called according to His purpose."

Unfortunately, Mrs Omwando did not have good news for Jessie when she replied to her letter. Her sister, Malkia was dead. Malkia's boyfriend ironically had murdered her in a fit of jealousy when he discovered that she was cheating on him.

Jessie broke down in her cell as memories of her sister flooded her mind. She asked God over and over to help her let go of the feelings of bitterness and betrayal. Then, slowly, she began to experience a transformation.

When Jessie surrendered her life to Jesus, she knew that she had a purpose –God's purpose. She began to feel a pressing desire to address the needs of her fellow prisoners. For one thing, the external environment of the prison was lacking in many ways. And so was the internal state of affairs in the hearts and minds of her fellow inmates. Many were trapped in guilt and shame; others, who were hardened criminals, had formed a thick wall around their hearts where they felt safe and that no one could penetrate. However, God had another plan; to use one of their own to change their lives forever. On Sundays when there was no external preacher available, Jessie began to share portions of scripture for a few minutes on Sundays. By and by, the prisoners began to take a keen interest in what Jessie was saying. On the first day, it had not been easy. Many had doubted the authenticity of her faith. It seemed impossible to them that a murderer could be forgiven.

"*Eti sasa wewe umeokoka?*" A huge woman called Atoti challenged her, insinuating that she did not believe Jessie was truly saved.

Through much prayer, Jessie had obtained favour with the prison warden, who had gifted her a Bible. It was an answered prayer to her hunger and thirst for the word, quite literally as expressed in the Beatitudes in the Bible by Jesus. "Blessed are those who hunger and thirst for righteousness, for they shall be filled." Jessie found herself poring over the Bible for hours. As a child, she had not had much access to a Bible as the readings were done in the church and very few of the flock carried personal Bibles with them. Now, she had time to read the Bible and meditate on it.

A new life had begun for Jessie. She was still in prison, but in her spirit, she was free. "Whom the Son sets free is free indeed," John 8:36.

Jessie could not have known then that God still had further surprises up His sleeve. The best was yet to come. Ten years had passed since Jessie's conversion to a new life in Christ. She never gave up hope but continued with her prison ministry, deriving much encouragement from the letters of St. Paul, as he had also known what it felt like to be in prison. One morning, the warden came excitedly to her cell.

"The chief warden wants to see you," she told Jessie.

Jessie splashed cold water on her face and hurried out when the police officer unlocked her cell door. She found an entire team waiting for her at the chief warden's office. It comprised a lawyer, three police officers, the warden, and the chief warden.

"What is this all about?" Jessie inquired, wondering why everyone was so happy.

"Jessie, *uko huru!*" One of the police officers told her. She looked in his direction in disbelief.

"What, why?" She was shell shocked.

"The president has pardoned you, among twenty other prisoners serving life imprisonment in the country. This is after careful analysis of best improved behaviour during the prison term."

The chief warden called the prison pastor to come and pray for her before she was released. She said goodbye to her fellow prisoners, many of whom had become her friends and to the staff. They gave her the same few belongings she had walked into prison with ten years ago - her watch, money and cell phone.

C H A P T E R 17

Jessie could taste the freedom as she stepped out into the crisp evening air. Her once elastic skin was now taut after years of negligence. It seemed hard to believe she had been in prison for over ten years. She walked about in a daze.

Jessie wondered what life as an ex-convict would look like; what it would be like to have a previously adoring public now know the ugly and grimy truth about her. She decided she would hold her head up high and live life as normally as she could, ignoring their curious and sometimes cold, hard stares. It was something she guessed she would have to live with for the rest of her life.

Jessie's clothes sagged against her lean frame, her body fighting to hold ground against the buffeting wind. She half expected to see her family running towards her – all trying to hug her at once. Then the mirage vanished, just as unexpectedly as it had come.

Suddenly, someone tall lunged at her from behind and grabbed her, knocking them both flat on the ground. Jessie was too shocked to respond, and the only words that came from her mouth were small, inaudible sounds. However, her assailant remained cool. He seemed unable to take his eyes off her, not even for a second. He had held her tight even as they repeatedly rolled to the other side of the road. "Let go of me!" She screamed into his ear, but he would not budge.

"You're going to burst my eardrums," His stern voice somehow made her shut up at once. Jessie could not imagine what anyone would want with an ex-convict.

Mr Mysterious finally released his vice-like grip, albeit reluctantly. "You're coming with me." He yanked a handful of her hair and started to drag her to a waiting white Toyota. A resounding slap shocked her temporarily out of her confounded state, when she began to scream. He bundled her into the boot, which was filled with old newspapers and some cranky toys. Jessie closed her eyes once more and tried to imagine this was not happening to her. They drove for what seemed like forever, but was really a little under two hours in reality. Finally, the car slowed down, and they turned into what sounded like a rough inner dirt road for a further five hundred metres. He tied her hands up this time, blindfolded her, and led her to a wooden shack. "You'll be here until the day you speak up." The words sent shock waves throughout her body.

What could he possibly mean? Jessie wondered, as she racked her brains for an answer but seemed to be experiencing a mental blackout and gave up trying. Jessie lay down on the wooden floor and fell into a deep, troubled sleep. She woke up screaming in the dark. Her captor woke up and was by her side in an instant. He laughed cruelly and slapped her.

"No one can hear you, even if you scream your lungs out."

Her screams gradually faded to whimpers as she realized this was most likely true. The mysterious men left soon after, leaving Jessie alone with her thoughts.

She had to formulate a plan to get out, fast. Wild ideas raced through her mind. However, depressing thoughts overtook them and she started crying. How had he managed to track her down, and just who was he anyway?

Jessie tried tugging at the cloth that tied her hands. It gave way immediately, almost as if he had been in such a hurry and had not cared if she succeeded in undoing the knot. She dashed madly out of her prison into the fresh air outside. It felt as though she could not stop running. She was never going to let anyone imprison her again in life – whether in a mental or physical prison.

Jessie finally had to stop to catch her breath. The whole ordeal seemed surreal. "From prison to prison," she thought. She wondered who would have expected such an event to occur to her – an ex-convict.

Unknown to Jessie, her captor had been one of John's relatives.

CHAPTER 18

Looking at the signs around her, Jessie realised she was in Machakos. She could not help wondering if her fate was due to some dark powers. Kambaland was, after all, rumoured to be the hub of mystics. However, several churches had mushroomed in the area in the recent years, with frequent vigils on Friday nights. Some welcomed this idea and embraced the Christian faith wholeheartedly; others felt it was an invasion of their private and personal space. Jessie knew that these 'victims' had called the government authorities several times to come and stop the Christian open-air crusades. She shuffled her dusty feet through a shopping centre, only stopping to buy some necessary supplies for her hosts. Unfortunately, her money was of very little value after all these years.

She had been fortunate to bump into an old friend when she escaped from her kidnapper. Despite the bruises on her face and emaciated body, her friend Mwikali and her husband Mwanzia had no objection to hosting her for a couple of weeks until she was back on her feet again. They were born-again Christians who fellowshipped in a nearby church where they introduced Jessie. They had also updated Jessie's parents about her whereabouts.

On this particular Friday, they had encouraged her to attend the New Year Kesha- an overnight vigil with them. Jessie could hear the sound of singing and clapping as they approached the church. She haltingly followed her friends. Everyone, it seemed, was praising God and lifting their hands, meting out hearty thanksgiving to their maker. She was not used to this kind of atmosphere in a church. Growing up, she went to a mainstream church where everything was done very quietly and with a lot of structure. She sang all their songs from hymn books, and she had never seen anyone raising their hands in worship.

Soon after, she had another experience that she would live to remember.

She found herself face to face with the pastor, a kind young man who gazed intently at her and told her about the power of the Holy Spirit. The handsome, young pastor happened to be the same one that led Jessie to Christ and was the leader of Bible Study in the church. His name was Jerome. She shuddered at the similarity of the names; John and Jerome. Jessie, however, found no comparison between the two men. One was cold, conniving, and calculating; the other was caring, cheerful, and charming.

Guilty feelings bombarded Jessie. How could she have such thoughts about a man of God? She, however, could not help wondering if he was single or perhaps a widower. Time would tell.

She was not in a hurry to start a new relationship when she already had so much going on in her life. On the flip side, he seemed to possess just about all of the qualities on her checklist; respectful to women, caring, tall, slim, effective communicator, organized, focused…Jessie pushed the stubborn thoughts of Pastor Jerome out of her head.

The service was electric. No one wanted to leave. Finally, it was dawn. Pastor Jerome asked people who had urgent needs to come forward. Jessi was one of them. He recognized her from her prison experience but did not mention it. Instead, he placed a reassuring hand on her shoulder and prayed earnestly for her. As she left the church with Mwikali and Mwanzia, Jessie felt a sense of great peace. She headed back to their home.

C H A P T E R 19

The next day, Mwanzia arrived home early from work with Mwikali. They expected to find Jessie already home and were surprised when she was not. Mwanzia's phone rang just then. He picked it up. As he listened to the person on the other end, his hands trembled, and his face contorted.

"No!" He screamed into the telephone. "Noooooo! You're lying!" He shouted at the person on the other end of the phone.

Mwikali grabbed her husband's hand in a vice-like grip. "What's happening?

"I'll tell you later, let's go!" Mwanzia said hurriedly, leaving the house, and jumped into his car without waiting to see if his wife was following him. Mwikali raced down the driveway and joined

Mwanzia in the car. He drove at a breakneck speed to hospital. Jessie lay deathly still beneath the white sheets.
Mwikali immediately broke down at the sight of her friend.

Pastor Jerome stepped forward.

"This is so that the power of God might be made manifest," he spoke softly but firmly.

Mwanzia and Mwikali nodded their heads slowly.

Moments later, a group of church members arrived. Soon after, Jessie's parents arrived, too. They told Mwanzia and Mwikali that they had been anticipating their daughter's visit, but instead they learnt that Jessie had been in an accident.

"What happened was unexpected. Jessie was having an evening stroll. While she was crossing the street, a car drove up and knocked her over."

Everyone gasped. "So, the driver is the one who brought my daughter to the hospital?" Mr Omwando asked.

"No. The driver sped off," Mwanzia responded, without lifting his eyes from Jessie's still form.

"We must get hold of this hit and run idiot!" Mr. Omwando yelled.

Jessie lay motionless. All eyes were now on her. Pastor Jerome held up his hand to motion for silence. Everyone fell deathly quiet. He began to pray. "Father, I thank you for the life of Jessie. I thank you that you have a good plan for her life. She shall live and not die." Jessie's eyelids began to flutter. Her lips moved, and an incoherent sound came out.

"Maji...nataka maji."

The pastor rushed to the hospital dispenser and brought her a glass of water. He then called for the nurse. She came running and immediately took a look at Jessie's vitals. Her pulse was now steady, and the reading on the heart machine changed.

Her chest began to rise and fall normally. The nurse grinned excitedly. Everyone simultaneously heaved a huge sigh of relief and then burst into laughter. Tears were streaming down Mwikali's cheeks. Pastor Jerome said another prayer – this time one of thanksgiving. A soft "amen" came from Jessie's lips. Again, everyone's eyes were on her.

"God is faithful," she whispered.

"Yes, he is," replied Pastor Jerome.

"It was so beautiful – the place where I had been. He took my hand and gave me a grand tour."

"H…. he?" Jerome stuttered, knowing inside him that Jessie had had a near death experience.

The group stayed in the hospital for thirty more minutes until the guard came and announced that visiting time was up. Pastor Jerome, however, requested a little more time with the patient. The guard, quick to please the man of God, allowed Pastor Jerome to stay on. "*Wacha sisi tukimbie*," Mwanzia said as he ushered the church group hurriedly out of the room.

The pastor sat on the chair beside Jessie.

They talked for an hour until he could see that she was running out of breath. Conversations exhausted her.

"You need to relax. I would love to pray for you if that's okay with you." Jerome's searched Jessie's eyes as he gently took her hand. Her eyelids fluttered as she leaned back into the bed and closed her eyes.

The following day, Pastor Jerome came to the hospital to help her with the discharge procedure. Mwanzia and his wife were busy and had not found it difficult to convince Pastor Jerome to take on the task. He was already in the ward by 8 a.m.

"How is my patient?" He beamed.

"Excited about leaving this place," Jessie replied, her voice groggy.

"Let me handle the paperwork and I will be right back." Pastor Jerome was gone, but true to his promise, he returned in less than an hour.

"All sorted," he informed her, looking triumphant. He noticed she was shivering.

"Here, put this on, and let's get out of here," he said, holding out the brown sweater he was wearing. They left the room and strode to his car. The pastor held the door open for her.

"So gentlemen still exist," she thought as she settled comfortably into her seat. A warmth she had not felt in a while washed over her.

Pastor Jerome turned on some soft worship music. They both relaxed and slipped into meditation mode.

The pastor's car was white with dark brown leather seats, the latest land cruiser. She immediately liked it, as she had a fondness for land cruisers. It was funny that she should be thinking about this now. Jessie concluded that it must be her coping mechanism.

Once they hit the road, he confessed how tired he was and only wanted to take a nap.

"Did you not get a good night's sleep?" Jessie inquired, surprised.

"Not really. Not when I have a patient." He was referring to her, but Jessie pretended not to notice.

"Do you have family around?" He changed the subject abruptly.

"My husband died," she said.

"I'm so sorry," he responded, not sounding as sorry as he would have liked.

In a few minutes, they arrived at Mwanzia's place.

Pastor Jerome helped her out of the car. He requested Jessie's phone number before he left.

"Wishing you a quick recovery, Jessie," he said.

"Thank you for your help, Pastor." Jessie bade him goodbye and quickly entered the house.

What were these crazy feelings she was having for the man of God? "God help me," she murmured.

Thankfully, Pastor Jerome was not married.

Later that evening, just as she was about to get into bed after a hot shower, she heard her telephone beep. It was a text from Pastor Jerome. "Arrived home safe. Blessed night."

Her heart was pounding as she texted back, "Good night."

Jessie did not stir until late the following morning, when the doorbell rang. She could hear voices in the distance. She crept out of bed, wrapped herself in a *kikoy* and quickly pulled on a t-shirt. Five minutes later, Mwikali was rapping on her bedroom door.

"Wake up, Jessie! We have company!"

"I'm already up. Could you give me a few minutes?" Jessie's voice had a twinge of agitation in it.

Mwikali was ashamed of herself for forgetting that this was the first day out of the hospital for her invalid friend.

When Jessie finally dressed and emerged from her bedroom, at first, she could not believe it when she saw who was standing in front of her.

"Surprise!" Mwikali's trademark smile warmed the room. Jessie was still in shock at the pastor's surprise visit.

"We will have a power breakfast to celebrate, and Pastor Jerome will pray for us again," she said.

"That sounds good. And hi there, sister Jessie!" " Given the events of the previous day, Pastor Jerome sounded very energetic. Jessie was not used to being referred to as a 'sister' by a man she had a crush on. Her first instinct was to throw her arms around him, but she remembered her manners and slowly held out her hand. He shook it gingerly, as though she was a china doll and it might break.

Mwikali retreated to the kitchen and emerged with pancakes and chai – with freshly ground ginger and some cinnamon spice. She placed some oranges and mangoes on a tray and carried them to the dining room.

They sat around the table and joined hands in prayer. Jessie found it difficult to concentrate while Pastor Jerome held her hand, but she tried to focus anyway. He thanked God again for healing her. By the time he had finished, everyone was very close to tears.

Pastor Jerome announced that he had to leave. He looked directly at Jessie.

"You look like you could use some fresh air. How about I let you rest today and pick you up tomorrow?"

She nodded shyly, aware of her friends observing her with interest.

He picked her up at 4:00pm and took her to a lovely coffee shop that he loved. They both ordered tea and *mandazis* as he inquired how she was feeling.

In the middle of their conversation, Pastor Jerome looked directly into her eyes.

"Have you been seeing anyone since your husband died?"

Jessie blushed and looked down shyly. "No."

Now it was her turn to question him. "What about you? Are you married?"

Pastor Jerome's eyes turned moist. "No. I was engaged to someone, but she bailed out on me at the last minute."

"I'm so sorry," Jessie said, unsure of how empathetic she felt.

Pastor Jerome proceeded to fungua roho. "I'd like to spend more time with you and get to know you," he said.

There was a long lapse of silence, like in the movies, as Jessie finally responded haltingly, "O….o…o kay."

Pastor Jerome felt like he wanted to sweep Jessie off her feet for saying yes. However, he restrained himself.

Soon after, Pastor Jerome and Jessie started dating. After six months of getting to know each other, it was evident to anyone who saw them together that they loved each other. However, dating a pastor was quite different for Jessie compared to her dating history. Pastor Jerome was humble and easy to be with. Jessie could be herself around him. He could hold a conversation with small children just as easily as he could with elderly people.

Jessie found herself involved in various ministry projects alongside Pastor Jerome. Then, one day, he invited her to accompany him to a youth retreat in Mombasa. Jessie was fond of young people; the positive vibes that oozed from them always left her feeling energized.

On the last day of the youth camp, everyone huddled around the bonfire the young men had built. Jessie and Pastor Jerome sat side by side. As the young people retired to bed one by one, they took the chance to speak candidly about their feelings towards each other.

God's blessings add no sorrow. Jessie thought to herself that Pastor Jerome was certainly no sorrow. He looked stunning in a grey suit and a fuchsia tie. He and the groomsmen had been waiting patiently and looked relieved when the bridal party arrived. Just like at her first wedding, Samantha and Wabi were part of the bridal party.

They swayed from side to side in an elegant dance of praise to the almighty God for engineering the wedding to happen finally. Finally, it was Jessie's turn to walk down the aisle. She paused at the door as she remembered her first wedding. John was waiting for her. She winced with pain at this memory, and no one noticed her plastic smile except Pastor Jerome. His eyes seemed to bore into her very soul. It would be challenging to be one of those wives who said they were 'fine' and their husbands believed them.

Pastor Jerome was also having flashbacks of his own. He had presided over more weddings than he could count, all the while posing a calm outward demeanour, which contradicted the deep ache and longing he felt inside. To be loved...to be the one whose hand the bride's hand slipped into. To be the one starting a new home. Now, it was his time. He thought of the politician who had coined the phrase "it's our time to eat", albeit with a negative connotation.

He smiled as he thought, "It's my time to wed."

Jessie's slender hand was finally in his. Pastor Jerome gripped it firmly, like he was afraid to let her go. which is how he felt. Jessie smiled up at him. All her ghosts disappeared when Pastor Jerome smiled back at her. Her parents were ecstatic and totally at peace with their daughter's choice. They presented the couple with a title deed as a wedding gift.

On their wedding night, Jessie and Pastor Jerome headed for their honeymoon. Pastor Jerome had rented a lovely tented cabin in Hawaii. This was their first time to be on the island. They were enjoying every bit of their time together.

Night crept in, chasing away all traces of the golden sun. Then, at last, it was evening. Finally, after a quiet but romantic dinner, they retired to bed.

Jessie was sitting on her grandmother's homestead in Kisii. She, Malkia, and other children were sitting around the fireplace listening to traditional folklore, wide-eyed and full of fear. Most of the stories and sayings seemed to spell out gruesome punishments for those who dared disregard the cultural norms. Grannie looked unfazed as she delved into the more horrific events of the story. Jessie's favourite was about a beautiful young girl and the giant — sort of like the Western tale of Beauty and the Beast. Unfortunately, the girl's brains did not match her beauty as she allowed the giant to eat her body parts one by one until only her nose was left. Jessie was fascinated and appalled at the girl's lack of wit and the talking nose that remained. Jessie could feel the warmth of the fireplace and some hot liquid trickling down her sides. It was reddish, and she could not quite tell whether it was a reflection from the fire.

The scene changed abruptly. Jessie found herself on the highway, conscious of how odd she looked with her bare feet and tattered clothes. She hesitatingly held up her left thumb.

Several cars flew past, oblivious to the out of place hitchhiker. Her lips were parched, and her head throbbed. Finally, Jessie decided to make a bolder move and step further into the road, which seemed more desperate than daring.

The accident happened as quickly as that of John. She could hear the voices of eyewitnesses as they narrated the story. They disclosed that she had seemed like a mentally disabled person, meandering dangerously onto the busy highway. An oncoming truck had seen her too late to stop. The driver tried frantically to slam the brakes, but instead, the huge machine rammed into her weak body, crushing her underneath its weight.

Jessie felt herself slipping away. More of the hot blood continued to flow out of her body.

She had finally arrived at her final destination, where she would have eternal freedom.

"What is it, my love?" Her husband was shaking her.

"Nothing, Jerome." It felt strange to no longer address him by his title.

He was not convinced at all.

"You were screaming in your dream, or should I say, nightmare."

"Oh, it was nothing serious, hun." Jessie struggled to maintain her composure, but her new husband saw right through her.

"It's about John!" she finally surrendered and burst into tears.

"John?"

"My former husband."

"Let me make you a cup of coffee as you tell me all about it. How does that sound?"

"Good."

They were soon seated on the front porch, sipping hot coffee and staring into the moonlit ocean. The tide was high, but the waves were quiet. Jessie soon relaxed and began her tale. Her husband's eyes got wider and wider, especially as she got to the part about John's betrayal. He could see she was emotionally disturbed and put his arm around her.

"I would never treat you like that, sweetie," he said lovingly.

"I know. I'm so blessed to have met someone like you."

She continued the story but conveniently left out the part about the murder. By the time she was done, it was 4:00 am, and they were both very sleepy.

"Thanks for sharing that part of your life with me, hun." Jerome looked truly grateful.

Jessie, however, felt uncomfortable about keeping anything from him. So, she had not told Pastor Jerome the whole story. He had no idea that he had just married a murderer.

The rest of the honeymoon was uneventful. They returned to Kenya after two weeks.

CHAPTER 21

They were back to everyday life in Machakos. Jessie felt like the honeymoon was too short. On the flip side, every day with her husband felt like a honeymoon. And she knew it was not just a romantic phase that would wear off. This was real. Pastor Jerome was more than she had ever envisioned a perfect husband to be. She could hardly compare him in any way to her deceased husband. There was definitely something different about being married to a Christian.

His demeanour was gracious and gentle, even when giving guidance and direction. John had been outrightly controlling. It always had to be his way or hit the highway. Jessie had learnt how to avoid his emotional outbursts by agreeing with everything he proposed. Any disagreement would have led to a bitter quarrel. Jessie was not aggressive and would do anything to keep the peace. As she mulled over all this in her head, she suddenly felt extremely fortunate.

Everything had gone on smoothly, with the couple happily settling into their new home in Machakos.

Until the nightmares started. They always ended the same way as the first one, when they were on their honeymoon. With blood oozing from her body after being in a terrible accident. Somehow, she could not to forget John's death and how he died. Horrible voices in her head kept mocking her.

"Murderer! Murderer!

She would wake up screaming and sticking her hands in her ears.

"No, no, noooooo! Stop it!"

Pastor Jerome could now clearly tell something was wrong, though he had had that feeling before their wedding. However, he had proceeded with the marriage because he knew that Jessie was a trustworthy person. Unfortunately, that trust would soon be betrayed.

From the first time she had the nightmare during their honeymoon, he had begun to pray for peace and calm to be restored in his wife's life.

One night, Pastor Jerome had a dream. Jessie was in a restaurant talking to a man who looked like a criminal. They were talking in low, hushed tones, as though they were making important plans. In the next scene, another man was driving a car when he suddenly had an accident. The dream ended with his wife replacing the man and oozing blood. He got up, sweating. Jessie was screaming again. This time, Pastor Jerome did not bother to persuade her to explain what she had been dreaming about. He already knew.

He calmly got up and led his wife by her hand to the kitchen. Pastor Jerome poured some warm milk into two cups and brought them to the kitchen counter, where they both sat on a pair of tall stools.

He looked straight into Jessie's eyes. "Tell me what happened, please," he urged Jessie. "Otherwise, we cannot build our marriage on mistrust."

Jessie knew he was serious. She decided to talk.

She told him everything. By the time she was done, it was already 6:00 am. Her husband got up and walked wordlessly to the bedroom, changed into his jogging suit, and left. He needed a brisk walk in the fresh air outside to clear his clogged mind. How could he have married a murderer? In retrospect, Jessie appeared to be too good to be true when he first met her. She was from an affluent background, yet so simple as a person: her beautiful face oozed innocence.

"No-o o!" he yelled. Luckily, there was no one in sight, as they would have mistaken him for a lunatic. The pastor broke into a run; he wanted to run away from all the madness and never come back.

Meanwhile, back home, his wife was praying earnestly. Jessie had no idea what was going through her husband's head, but she knew she could not afford to have her second marriage broken.

She hoped that he was not walking out of her life with all her heart.

Jessie decided to turn to the only solution that seemed to be working a lot these days: Prayer. It was two hours before she felt she had unburdened her all to God. Just then, Pastor Jerome walked in with wide, open arms. He told her he had been praying too. God asked him to forgive her. It seemed impossible, but after two hours of inner struggle, Pastor Jerome gave in. After all, God had paid a much higher price so that sinful humankind could be forgiven and saved by a sinless man who did not deserve such punishment. Who was Pastor Jerome to hold back? They embraced, soaking each other in a torrent of tears.

Jessie felt free at last. There was, after all, a flip side to betrayal.

EPILOGUE

Betrayal is a bitter pill to swallow. It can cause deep seated bitterness, a bitterness that worms its way into the spirit, eating away at the soul like an acid. Jessie had fallen prey to this evil seed and allowed it to take root in her life. Her whole life is turned around completely as a result of being betrayed by her first husband and sister.

The Flip Side of Betrayal shows us that there can be a positive side to betrayal. It took the hand of a merciful God to reach into Jessie's heart and wrench out its ugliness. From ashes to beauty, Jessie becomes a new woman after this heart surgery. Indeed, God made all things beautiful for Jessie, in His own time.

She eventually lets go of the baggage from her troubled past and embarks on an exciting journey to make a new discovery. Not one of self-discovery, but Christ-discovery. Her true repentance and consequent salvation take her on a different path that is heaven bound.

2 Corinthians 5:17: "Therefore, if anyone is in Christ, he is a new creation; old things have passed away; behold, all things have become new."

Dear reader, as you share in this journey, may your self-reflection bring you to a place of insightful enlightenment as well as Christ reflection.

Blessings

Jean

GLOSSARY OF TERMS:

1. Mbogo Nduiki - In Kikuyu language means the lone bull; which is a very dangerous animal when provoked
2. Kitenge is an African wax print fabric that is usually colourful.
3. Bi-polar disorder - https://www.healthline.com/health/bipolar-disorder